Dead W

MW01125017

This is a work of fiction.

None of it is real. All names, places, and events are products of the author's imagination. Any resemblance to real names, places, or events are purely coincidental, and should not be construed as being real.

Dead Wrong
Copyright © 2013
Leighann Dobbs
http://www.leighanndobbs.com
All Rights Reserved.

No part of this work may be used or reproduced in any manner, except as allowable under "fair use," without the express written permission of the author.

Cover art by: http://www.coverkicks.com

More Books By This Author:

Lexy Baker
Cozy Mystery Series
* * *

Killer Cupcakes
Dying For Danish
Murder, Money and Marzipan
3 Bodies and a Biscotti
Brownies, Bodies & Bad Guys
Wedded Blintz

Blackmoore Sisters
Cozy Mystery Series
* * *

Dead Wrong
Dead & Buried
Dead Tide
Buried Secrets

Contemporary
Romance
* * *

Sweet Escapes
Reluctant Romance

Chapter One

Morgan Blackmoore tapped her finger lightly on the counter, her mind barely registering the low buzz of voices behind her in the crowded coffee shop as she mentally prioritized the tasks that awaited her back at her own store.

"Here you go, one yerba mate tea and a vanilla latte." Felicity rang up the purchase, as Morgan dug in the front pocket of her faded denim jeans for some cash which she traded for the two paper cups.

Inhaling the spicy aroma of the tea, she turned to leave, her long, silky black hair swinging behind her. Elbowing her way through the crowd, she headed toward the door. At this time of morning, the coffee shop was filled with locals and Morgan knew almost all of them well enough to exchange a quick greeting or nod.

Suddenly a short, stout figure appeared, blocking her path. Morgan let out a sharp breath, recognizing the figure as Prudence Littlefield.

Prudence had a long running feud with the Blackmoore's which dated back to some sort of run-in she'd had with Morgan's grandmother when they were young girls. As a result, Prudence loved to harass and berate the Blackmoore girls in public. Morgan's eyes darted around the room, looking for an escape route.

"Just who do you think you are?" Prudence demanded, her hands fisted on her hips, legs spaced shoulder width apart. Morgan noticed she was wearing her usual knee high rubber boots and an orange sunflower scarf.

Morgan's brow furrowed over her ice blue eyes as she stared at the older woman's prune like face.

"Excuse me?"

"Don't you play dumb with me Morgan Blackmoore. What kind of concoction did you give my Ed? He's been acting plumb crazy."

Morgan thought back over the previous week's customers. Ed Littlefield *had* come into her herbal remedies shop, but she'd be damned if she'd announce to the whole town what he was after.

She narrowed her eyes at Prudence. "That's between me and Ed."

Prudence's cheeks turned crimson. Her nostrils flared. "You know what *I* think," she said narrowing her eyes and leaning in toward Morgan, "I think you're a witch, just like your great-great-great-grandmother!"

Morgan felt an angry heat course through her veins. There was nothing she hated more than being called a witch. She was a Doctor of Pharmacology with a Master Herbalist's license, not some sort of spell-casting conjurer.

The coffee shop had grown silent. Morgan could feel the crowd staring at her. She leaned forward, looking wrinkled old Prudence Littlefield straight in the eye.

"Well now, I think we know that's not true," she said, her voice barely above a whisper, "Because if I was a witch, I'd have turned you into a newt long ago."

Then she pushed her way past the old crone and fled out the coffee shop door.

***

Fiona Blackmoore stared at the amethyst crystal in front of her wondering how to work it into a pendant. On most days, she could easily figure out exactly how to cut and position the stone, but right now her brain was in a pre-caffeine fog.

Where was Morgan with her latte?

She sighed, looking at her watch. It was ten past eight, Morgan should be here by now, she thought impatiently.

Fiona looked around the small shop, *Sticks and Stones*, she shared with her sister. An old cottage that had been in the family for generations, it sat at one of the highest points in their town of Noquitt, Maine.

Turning in her chair, she looked out the back window. In between the tree trunks that made up a small patch of woods, she had a bird's eye view of the sparkling, sapphire blue Atlantic Ocean in the distance.

The cottage sat about 500 feet inland at the top of a high cliff that plunged into the Atlantic. If the woods were cleared, like the developers wanted, the view would be even better. But Fiona would have none of that, no matter how much the developers offered them, or how much they needed the money. Her and her sisters would never sell the cottage.

She turned away from the window and surveyed the inside of the shop. One side was setup as an apothecary of sorts. Antique slotted shelves loaded with various herbs lined the walls. Dried weeds hung from the rafters and several mortar and pestles stood on the counter, ready for whatever herbal concoctions her sister was hired to make.

On her side sat a variety of gemologist tools and a large assortment of crystals. Three antique oak and glass jewelry cases displayed her creations. Fiona smiled as she looked at them. Since childhood she had been fascinated with rocks and gems so it was no surprise to anyone when she grew up to become a gemologist and jewelry designer, creating jewelry not only for its beauty, but also for its healing properties.

The two sisters vocations suited each other perfectly and they often worked together providing customers with crystal and herbal healing for whatever ailed them.

The jangling of the bell over the door brought her attention to the front of the shop. She breathed a sigh of relief when Morgan burst through the door, her cheeks flushed, holding two steaming paper cups.

"What's the matter?" Fiona held her hand out, accepting the drink gratefully. Peeling back the plastic tab, she inhaled the sweet vanilla scent of the latte.

"I just had a run in with Prudence Littlefield!" Morgan's eyes flashed with anger.

"Oh? I saw her walking down Shore road this morning wearing that god-awful orange sunflower scarf. What was the run-in about this time?" Fiona took the first sip of her latte, closing her eyes and waiting for the caffeine to power her blood stream. She'd had her own run-ins with Pru Littlefield and had learned to take them in stride.

"She was upset about an herbal mix I made for Ed. She called me a witch!"

"What did you make for him?"

"Just some Ginkgo, Ginseng and Horny Goat Weed ... although the latter he said was for Prudence."

Fiona's eyes grew wide. "Aren't those herbs for impotence?"

Morgan shrugged "Well, that's what he wanted."

"No wonder Prudence was mad... although you'd think just being married to her would have caused the impotence."

Morgan burst out laughing. "No kidding. I had to question his sanity when he asked me for it. I thought maybe he had a girlfriend on the side."

Fiona shook her head trying to clear the unwanted images of Ed and Prudence Littlefield together.

"Well, I wouldn't let it ruin my day. You know how *she* is."

Morgan put her tea on the counter, then turned to her apothecary shelf and picked several herbs out of the slots. "I know, but she always seems to know how to push my buttons. Especially when she calls me a witch."

Fiona grimaced. "Right, well I wish we *were* witches. Then we could just conjure up some money and not be scrambling to pay the taxes on this shop and the house."

Morgan sat in a tall chair behind the counter and proceeded to measure dried herbs into a mortar.

"I know. I saw Eli Stark in town yesterday and he was pestering me about selling the shop again."

"What did you tell him?"

"I told him we'd sell over our dead bodies." Morgan picked up a pestle and started grinding away at the herbs.

Fiona smiled. Eli Stark had been after them for almost a year to sell the small piece of land their shop sat on. He had visions of buying it, along with some adjacent lots in order to develop the area into high end condos.

Even though their parents early deaths had left Fiona, Morgan and their two other sisters property rich but cash poor the four of them agreed they would never sell. Both the small shop and the stately ocean home they lived in had been in the family for generations and they didn't want *their* generation to be the one that lost them.

The only problem was, although they owned the properties outright, the taxes were astronomical and, on their meager earnings, they were all just scraping by to make ends meet.

All the more reason to get this necklace finished so I can get paid. Thankfully, the caffeine had finally cleared the cobwebs in her head and Fiona was ready to get to work. Staring down at the amethyst, a vision of the perfect shape to cut the stone appeared in her mind. She grabbed her tools and started shaping the stone.

Fiona and Morgan were both lost in their work. They worked silently, the only sounds in the little shop being the scrape of mortar on pestle and the hum of Fiona's gem grinding tool mixed with a few melodic tweets and chirps that floated in from the open window.

Fiona didn't know how long they were working like that when the bell over the shop door chimed again. She figured it must have been an hour or two judging by the fact that the few sips left in the bottom of her latte cup had grown cold.

She smiled, looking up from her work to greet their potential customer, but the smile froze on her face when she saw who it was.

Sheriff Overton stood in the door flanked by two police officers. A toothpick jutted out of the side of Overton's mouth and judging by the looks on all three of their faces, they weren't there to buy herbs or crystals.

Fiona could almost hear her heart beating in the silence as the men stood there, adjusting their eyes to the light and getting their bearings.

"Can we help you?" Morgan asked, stopping her work to wipe her hands on a towel.

Overton's head swiveled in her direction like a hawk spying a rabbit in a field.

"That's her." He nodded to the two uniformed men who approached Morgan hesitantly. Fiona recognized one of the men as Brody Hunter, whose older brother Morgan had dated all through high school. She saw Brody look questioningly at the Sheriff.

The other man stood a head taller than Brody. Fiona noticed his dark hair and broad shoulders but her assessment of him stopped there when she saw him pulling out a pair of handcuffs.

Her heart lurched at the look of panic on her sister's face as the men advanced toward her.

"Just what is this all about?" She demanded, standing up and taking a step toward the Sheriff.

There was no love lost between the Sheriff and Fiona. They'd had a few run-ins and she thought he was an egotistical bore and probably crooked too. He ignored her question focusing his attention on Morgan. The next words out of his mouth chilled Fiona to the core.

"Morgan Blackmoore ... you're under arrest for the murder of Prudence Littlefield."

Chapter Two

"Just what is the meaning of this?" Fiona stepped closer to the Sheriff. The smell of stale cigarettes kept her a few paces from getting right in his face.

She felt her stomach curdle as he turned his rheumy eyes on her. The ever-present toothpick bobbed up and down. "Mrs. Littlefield was found not one quarter mile from here. Murdered."

"And what makes you think my sister did it?" She demanded, hands on hips.

"Earlier this morning, Morgan was overheard telling Prudence that she wanted to turn her into a newt."

Fiona wrinkled her brow. "So?"

"Prudence was found with a newt stuffed in her throat. She'd been strangled." He turned to face Morgan. "Where were you two hours ago?"

The girls exchanged glances and Fiona looked at her watch. Two hours ago was about when she was waiting for Morgan to come back with her coffee.

"I was walking here from the coffee shop," Morgan said. "And I didn't say I wanted to turn her into a newt, I said *if* I was a witch I would have *already* turned her into a newt."

"Close enough for me," Sheriff Overton said. "Did anyone see you walking here?"

"Surely, you can't be serious?" Morgan stared at him incredulously. "That's just the kind of thing you say when someone pisses you off. You can't seriously think I actually killed her over a small argument in a coffee shop?"

"That remains to be seen." Overton nodded at the officers. "Cuff her and get her into the car." He switched the toothpick from one side of his mouth to the other, then snickered at Fiona before turning and walking out of the shop.

Fiona stared at his retreating back, trying to get her mouth to work. She whirled around at the sound of snapping handcuffs, planting herself firmly in between the officers and the door.

"You can't just arrest her like this. You need more solid evidence!" She glared at the two men.

Brody looked down at the floor.

"That's right Brody Hunter, you should be ashamed of yourself." She turned her steely blue gaze on the other officer.

"And you, whoever you are. How dare you come to our town and arrest my sister on this flimsy evidence. I'll have you brought up under charges of false arrest!"

Fiona was standing close to him; his height forced her to tilt her head backwards to look up into his face. She saw his gray eyes soften a little before he gently moved her aside.

"Sorry Ma'am," he dipped his head at her, "Just doing my job." Then he brushed past her, tugging Morgan along behind him.

Fiona stomped outside after them. She noticed with annoyance that they'd parked the police car sideways in the front lawn instead of just leaving it in the driveway. She stood at the side of the car, her fists clenched so hard that her nails dug into her palms painfully, and watched them put Morgan in the back seat.

Bending down, she looked in through the window at her sister. "Don't worry Morgan, they can't do this. I'll be right down to get you out."

Overton walked by, pushing her aside and the three men piled into the car; Brodie and Overton in the front and the other officer in the back with Morgan. Overton started the car and sped off, digging up a piece of their front yard with his back tire.

Fiona's heart lurched as she saw Morgan turn her head and look out the back window at her. She spun around and raced back into the store, her heart pounding in her chest. Grabbing her purse, she locked up the shop and ran to her twelve year old pick-up truck.

Mumbling a prayer to the car starting gods, she held her breath while she pumped the gas pedal and turned the key in the ignition. Relief flooded her when the old truck sputtered to life and she jammed it into drive and peeled out, pointing the truck in the direction of the police station.

***

Fiona burst through the door to the police station, her curly red hair flying wildly behind her. Storming over to the counter, she pounded on the top catching the attention of George O'Neil who gave her a sympathetic look.

"I demand to see my sister," she yelled, accentuating the words by pounding on the counter even louder.

George took a step back and held his hands up, palms out. "Whoa there, Fiona, I know you're upset but you need to calm down."

"I'll handle this, George." Someone said from behind her and she whirled around to confront him. It was the officer that had arrested Morgan, the one she'd never seen before.

Fiona had heard talk that some fancy cop from Boston had taken a job on their small town police force, which was strange because most cops were trying to get out of Noquitt and move to the big city. Not too many people moved *to* Noquitt from other places and Fiona had an instant distrust of anyone who did. *Probably some big scandal in his past or maybe Overton had brought him in to help corrupt the town.*

"Just who *are* you?" She narrowed her eyes at him.

"Jake Cooper."

Fiona eyed the hand he stuck out at her suspiciously, then placed her own hand inside it. His handshake was firm, his hand large and calloused. She had to admit the feeling wasn't all too unpleasant, but she didn't have time to dwell on that—she was on a mission.

"And you are?" He prompted.

She ripped her hand away. "Fiona Blackmoore ...and I want to see my sister *now*."

"I'm sorry, but she's being processed. You can't see her until visiting hours at 5 pm," he said softly.

"What do you mean I can't see her? You can't just keep her in there alone ... I mean, doesn't she get a phone call or something?" Fiona blinked away tears of frustration.

"I'm sorry," Jake spread his hands. "That's the rule. I promise you she's being treated well ... I mean, heck, she seems to be old friends with everyone back there. They'll take good care of her."

Jake's soothing tone and words of comfort had the opposite effect on Fiona. She felt her anger rising and took a step closer to him.

"Look buddy, I don't know what's going on here or who you people think you are, but I do know that you can't arrest my sister on this flimsy evidence." Fiona wondered if they had some other evidence they had not told her about, but brushed away the thought. She *knew* Morgan didn't kill Prudence.

She saw a flicker of something in Jake's eyes. Understanding? Guilt? Compassion? He leaned in toward her, lowering his voice.

"Listen, if I were you, I'd go home and calm down. Get a decent lawyer. Then come back this afternoon and you should be able to get her out," he said glancing over at the desk as if to make sure no one heard him.

Fiona was taken aback. Was he trying to help her? Or was this all part of their trap? Suddenly she felt alone, confused and helpless. *Why were they trying to blame this on Morgan?*

"I don't know what you people are up to," she said, taking a step closer to the tall officer. "But if you think my sister did this you are *dead wrong.*"

She punctuated the last two words by poking her index finger hard at his chest, her eyes widening in surprise at the solid muscle she felt. *Or was that his kevlar vest?* Jerking her finger away before she could contemplate it further, she turned and fled out of the station.

Flinging open the door to her truck she tumbled inside, shaking so hard she could barely get her key in the ignition. As she drove away she remembered what Jake had said about getting a lawyer. She knew a good one and wanted the best chance for Morgan, but lawyers didn't come cheap nor did they work for free.

Chewing her bottom lip, she wondered how on earth they would pay for a lawyer when they could barely raise the money to pay the taxes on their home.

Her stomach felt like lead as she drove toward town on autopilot. Her mind was so busy trying to work a solution that she barely noticed how crowded the roads were getting now that tourist season had started. Or how all the shops were now opening for the season. Or Mrs. Penobscott setting up for her perpetual weekend yard sale that she stocked with random items she found in the attic of her old family home.

Suddenly Fiona had an idea of how she could get the money to hire a lawyer for Morgan. She pressed harder on the gas and headed toward home.

Chapter Three

The springs on Jake's ancient police-issue chair protested loudly as he leaned back and put his feet on the desk. He knew the woman in the holding cell was no murderer. He had a gut instinct about these things, and he was usually right. Of course, getting Sheriff Overton to see it his way was another story.

It was curious, though, that Overton had been so adamant about arresting her, even though any fool could see the evidence was circumstantial at best. But then, Overton rarely did things that made sense to Jake.

Jake ran his hand over the stubble on his chin. He hated to admit it, but he just didn't get a warm feeling about his new boss. Something was strange about him. Jake often found him difficult to work with. Overton was the type of guy that was never wrong, and some of the things he did made Jake wonder which side of the law he was on. But Jake was the new guy ... a peon, so he just nodded and did his job.

Of course, he wouldn't just stand by and let Overton prosecute someone without the proper evidence, but hopefully it wouldn't come to that. Surely the various lawyers and judges involved would laugh in Overton's face if he tried to get a trial on the evidence he had ... which made Jake wonder just what the Sheriff was up to with this arrest.

He'd almost refused to handcuff Morgan, but something told him it would be better if he played along. Still, he'd felt bad snapping those metal shackles on her slender wrist. At least he'd made sure they were loose—she probably could have wriggled out of them if she'd tried. But she didn't.

Jake smiled thinking of the redheaded sister and how fiercely she had tried to defend Morgan. She sure was a feisty one, whereas the dark haired girl was more calm; serene almost. The two were so different. You'd never know they were sisters, except they both had those piercing ice-blue eyes.

Jake had always been a sucker for redheads but he had no intention of getting caught up in any kind of relationship.

Especially not in a small town like Noquitt where everybody knew everybody else's business. Besides, he'd had enough of relationships to last him a lifetime in Boston.

Probably better off to avoid the Blackmoore sisters ... and maybe even the whole case.

Still, he felt bad for the woman sitting in the jail cell in the basement of the police station. She didn't have any prior arrest record, so she was probably terrified. Not to mention she was most likely there under false pretenses. Jake couldn't do anything about that, but he could do something to make her stay a little less harrowing.

He slid his feet off the desk, slapping them down on the floor and picked up his phone to dial in some take-out. The least he could do was get her something decent to eat besides the slop they'd give her down there.

He placed the order for a pot-roast dinner to be delivered at five. He planned to take it down to her himself for dinner, convincing himself he was just doing a good deed to try to make up for his role in her arrest and it had nothing to do with the fact that her sister would be back just around supper time.

Chapter Four

Fiona's heart thumped in her chest. She stared at the old door that led to the attic. Reaching for the glass knob, she turned it slowly. The squeaking of the hinges echoed loudly in the stairwell setting her nerves on edge.

The stairs loomed in front of her, stretching up into the darkness of the fourth floor. Fumbling for a light switch, she took a deep breath. It was silly to be afraid of the attic. After all, it was just a big room ... well, more than a room as it comprised the whole fourth floor of the mansion her and her sisters lived in. But she had been warned since childhood by her mother and grandmother to stay away from there and the place still scared her even if she was all grown up now.

Of course, Fiona and her sisters had ignored the warning on several occasions, but every time she had gone in there she'd felt creeped out and never stayed long.

Today, she *had* to go in. Morgan's freedom depended on it.

Ascending the stairs cautiously, she cringed as the old, dry wood creaked and groaned as if protesting her presence. The temperature rose a notch with each step she took and she felt thankful it was mid-spring and not summer when the attic heat would be unbearable.

She swiveled her head at the top of the stairs, trying to decide where to start. The attic, which had been servant's quarters hundreds of years ago, held a maze of rooms and cubby holes which were packed with the cast-offs of her ancestors. Two hundred and seventy five years of household and personal belongings gathered dust up here.

Did her people never throw anything away?

Breathing in the smell of old wood, she started picking out a path toward the back of the house. Sunlight filtered in through the windows highlighting the dust motes hanging in the still, dry air.

She wasn't sure exactly what she was looking for. Something they could sell, pawn or trade to raise the money for a lawyer. Even though they had made a pact to never sell any of their family heirlooms, Fiona felt certain her other sisters would agree to make the exception for Morgan.

She turned her head from side to side, slowly navigating the attic. Her breath caught suddenly in her throat when she spied a human figure out of the corner of her eye. Then she released it just as quickly when she realized it was just an old dress form.

Passing old trunks, rolled up rugs, closed up boxes, dinnerware, furniture and even a kitchen sink, she realized she'd never really looked at any of the stuff in the attic and slowly became mesmerized with the task.

Crash!

Fiona's heart exploded in her chest and she whirled around toward the direction of the noise, her fists tight at her side. Her eyes searched rapidly for some sort of weapon. Her mind raced. *Who would be up in the attic with her?*

"Meow."

Fiona let her breath out sharply, her shoulders relaxed.

"Belladonna, you scared the heck out of me."

She bent to pick up the cream and white cat. "What are you doing up here?" She asked, stroking her fur. Belladonna answered with a purr.

"Probably hunting for mice," Fiona mused.

Setting the cat down she noticed what had made the noise. A heavy book lay on the floor, a century of dust floating in the air around it.

Belladonna must have knocked the book off.

Fiona went over and picked the book off the floor, taking care not to crack the leather binding. Setting it gently on a nearby table, she stared at the pages. They looked ancient, like parchment, the ink on them faded almost to nothing. Carefully she turned a page, hoping her touch didn't cause the fragile paper to disintegrate.

The book looked like some sort of journal; the ink clearly from a quill pen, the words barely legible. *Could this be one of her ancestor's sailing journals?*

According to family legend, the main part of their home had been built in the early 1700's by a merchant who sailed the world. The house itself, sat on a large cliff with the ocean on two sides and the entrance to Perkins Cove on the third ... A perfect location for a sailing man.

The house had been added to over the centuries, finally becoming a massive Victorian mansion, but the main part of the house still was within the structure and she'd heard her mother and grandmother talk about old journals from the original builder of the house.

She frowned down at the old book. She couldn't make out any dates and it seemed a book that old would have been further toward the back. Tiny pin pricks on her leg interrupted her thoughts. She looked down to see Belladonna scratching at her.

"Right, I'm up here to look for something to help Morgan, not read some old journals, thanks for reminding me." She carefully closed the book and put it back in its place in the bookshelf, mentally cataloging the location so she could revisit it later when she had more time.

Apparently satisfied, Belladonna wound her way around Fiona's leg and scampered off with a tiny "Mew."

Fiona started to continue her search but was interrupted by a series of meows. *Had Belladonna gotten stuck somewhere? Was she hurt?* Her meows certainly sounded pitiful to Fiona's ears.

Following the sound, she came to a small cut out in the eaves. The area was well lit by a large window through which she could see the dark blue ocean. An old rocking chair sat under the window and Fiona felt relieved to see Belladonna was unharmed. The small cat crouched on the floor in front of the chair batting around a shiny object.

"What do you have there?"

"Mew!" Belladonna cast her ice-blue eyes up at Fiona before returning her attention to the shiny object which she batted in Fiona's direction.

Fiona bent to pick it up, watching it sparkle in the light. Spreading it out in her hands she realized it was a necklace. She recognized the style as being popular in the mid 1800's … probably one of her great-great-great-grandmothers pieces that had been stored up here after her death.

Fiona could tell it was well made—this was no junky piece of costume jewelry. Which was odd, because she was under the impression that nothing of real value was up here. Her mother had always said it was just a bunch of old broken junk the family was too miserly to throw away.

But where did it come from? She looked around the floor for a jewelry box or some sort of container it might have been in but saw nothing.

The glitter of the light from the window reflecting off the stones in the necklace caught her eye and she moved closer to the window to look at it in the light. Squinting, she held the necklace up to the glass looking for the tell-tale signs that the stones were worthless paste or glass. *Why hadn't she thought to bring a jewelers loupe?*

Her training as a gemologist had given her a keen eye and the knowledge to be able to tell a gemstone from a fake. Naturally tools helped her validate her assessment, but with the naked eye it appeared this necklace was the real deal ... diamonds, emeralds and gold.

Fiona's heart flipped in her chest and she felt like a huge weight had been lifted from her shoulders. If the necklace tested to be real, it would be worth much more than what she needed to secure a lawyer for Morgan.

Clutching the jewelry in her hand, she turned and ran toward the stairs. She knew exactly what to do with the necklace to get the money they needed without having to sell off a potentially important family heirloom. She just hoped her sisters were home so she could discuss her plan with them and get their approval in time to put the wheels in motion before it was too late to save Morgan from spending the night in jail.

Chapter Five

The back stairs dumped Fiona out into the black and white tiled kitchen where Belladonna stood at her food bowl, munching away. Fiona frowned at the cat wondering how she had beat her to the kitchen without passing her on the stairs as she raced over to the pantry to get her test kit.

"*There* you are." Celeste appeared in the doorway and Fiona noticed the worry on her face. "I heard about Morgan in town so I put Diana in charge of the yoga studio and came right home. I yelled all over the house for you, but you didn't answer. Where *were* you?"

Fiona turned holding up the necklace, "In the attic."

Celeste looked at the ceiling. "You went up there alone?"

"It was the only way I could think of to find something we could use to secure a lawyer for Morgan. It's not so bad up there, really." Fiona shrugged.

Fiona took her test kit and the necklace back into the kitchen and set them on the large island in the center. The spacious kitchen had been built sometime in the mid-1800s and still had the original dark cabinets offset by white marble counters. Stainless steel appliances were a newer addition as was the island which had a sink in the center. It had chairs setup on one side and the sisters spent many hours there, chatting and eating.

"So, what happened with Morgan?" Celeste plopped herself down cross legged in the chair on the other side of the island. She ran her hand nervously through her short white-blonde hair while Fiona recounted the mornings events.

"She's still in jail? Can they even do that without concrete evidence?" Celeste's ice-blue eyes narrowed and she worried her bottom lip.

"I don't know if they *can*, but they *have*. Sheriff Overton doesn't seem to like us much."

"Tell me about it," Celeste said, making a face. "But the new guy, Jake I think his name is, seems kind of nice."

Fiona felt her stomach do a little flip at the mention of Jake. *What was that all about?* She ignored it and started cleaning off a section of the necklace, then clipped the alligator clip from her gold tester to it.

"So what's up with the necklace?" Celeste asked.

"We need to get Morgan a lawyer, but, since we have no money, I thought maybe we could find something in the attic we could sell ..." Fiona let her voice trail off and looked up to judge Celeste's reaction but her sister retained her usual calm demeanor.

"It sure is pretty," Celeste said, leaning over the island to get a better look. "I wonder which one of our relatives it belonged to."

Fiona didn't have an answer, so she turned the gold tester on and filled the well with testing acid, then dipped the section of necklace in. Both sisters held their breath while they waited for the machine to tell them if it was real gold or not.

Fiona felt her heart skip a beat when the machine beeped and the light lit up. The necklace was 18K gold.

"Nice!" Celeste raised her hand up and Fiona slapped her palm in a high five.

"So what's your plan?"

Fiona looked up from the task of packing up the test kit. "I think I know how we can raise the money for Morgan's lawyer without actually having to sell the necklace, but I need you and Jolene to give it the thumbs up," she said. "Where is our little sister?"

Celeste pushed her brows together. "I haven't seen her."

Fiona bit her lower lip. Her youngest sister, Jolene, had been a hand full since their mother had jumped to her death from the cliff behind their house four years ago. The poor girl had only been fourteen. It had affected all the girls deeply, but Jolene was hurt the most at her young age.

Fiona, Celeste and Morgan had tried to raise her as best they could, but Celeste had only been nineteen, herself. Morgan and Fiona had been in their late twenties and had tried to share the role of mothering between them.

Jolene had been a terror in her teenage years, which likely contributed to the dislike Sheriff Overton had for the whole family. But since she'd turned eighteen a few months ago, Fiona had started to see a change in her. She guessed she was finally growing up.

Still, it worried her that they didn't know where Jolene was, she was supposed to either be home or let one of them know where she was if she went out.

As if summoned by magic, Jolene suddenly came sauntering in from the living room, head down, bopping to the music that blared so loudly from her ear buds that Fiona could hear it on the other side of the room.

Fiona felt a nudge of annoyance when the girl didn't even look up at either of them.

"Jolene," she said but the girl continued on her path to the pantry without even stopping.

"*Jolene!*" Fiona yelled eliciting a startled look from the teen who swiveled her head in

Fiona's direction, then reached up to pull out an ear bud.

"Oh. Hi. Sorry, didn't see you there." Jolene shrugged an apology then shifted her gaze between her two sisters. "Wassup?"

"It's about Morgan." Fiona saw Jolene's eyes grow wide. The ice-blue color looked startling against her pale face and chocolate brown hair. Fiona marveled at how all four of the sisters had the same color eyes — a family trait shared by many Blackmoore women — but all had different hair and coloring.

"What? Did something happen to her?" Jolene swiveled her head between the two sisters.

"Sort of," Fiona said. Then she repeated the story of Morgan's arrest while Jolene listened intently, her frown growing deeper and deeper.

"They're keeping her in jail? That Overton is really a jerk."

Normally Fiona would have told her not to say bad things about others, but this time she couldn't really argue, he *was* a jerk.

"Don't worry. We're getting her out this afternoon. I want to hire Delphine Jones to represent Morgan, but she needs a $5000 retainer just to take the case."

Celeste gasped. "Where are we going to get five grand?"

"That's where this comes in." Fiona held the necklace up, dangling it from her fingers.

Jolene raised her eyebrows. "Where'd you get that?"

"In the attic."

Fiona saw Jolene shudder. "Mom always told me the most horrid ghost stories of the attic, I was always afraid to go up there."

Fiona felt her heart ache at the mention of her mother. Tears pricked the backs of her eyes as she remembered the colorful stories of their ancestors including tales of pirates, witches and ghostly hauntings that their mother had loved to tell. Fiona knew they were all mostly "made-up" but, as a child, she had listened to each one with rapt attention.

"So, you want to sell it?" Celeste interrupted her thoughts.

"No, not sell it. Pawn it," Fiona said. "We can take it down to Cal Reed and see if he'll take it in exchange for the money we need. We know the charges against Morgan will never stick. She didn't do it. So we won't need to spend the whole five grand with Delphine. Once Morgan is cleared, we can get the rest of our deposit back, scrape up whatever we need to top it off to five thousand, and collect the necklace from Cal."

"That's a great idea. We know we can trust Cal," Celeste said.

Calvin Reed had been a classmate of Fiona's and good friends with all the Blackmoore girls since they were kids. He was practically like a brother to them. Fiona had no doubt he would take good care of their necklace in his pawn shop. It was the best way she could think of to raise the money and still have a chance of keeping the necklace in the family.

"So, are we in agreement to do this?" Fiona asked.

"Yes!"

"Of course!"

"Great." Fiona put her fisted hand out toward the other girls, her knuckles facing them and the three did a knuckle tap.

"If you need to come up with more money, I have a little socked away from my job," Jolene said. Having recently graduated, she'd taken a job at one of the local restaurants, *Barnacle Bill's*, until she decided what she wanted to do with her life.

Fiona felt her heart melt at the offer. A year ago, it seemed like Jolene could have cared less what happened to any of them. She was distant and moody, spending most of her time in her room or arguing with them. But she really seemed to be coming around. Fiona wondered if this was how a parent felt when they realized their little child was finally growing up.

"Hopefully it won't come to that," Fiona said. "Now let's get a move on. We still have to meet with Delphine and go over to Cal's. I don't want Morgan rotting in jail any longer than she has to."

Chapter Six

"I'm going to give Overton a piece of my mind," sputtered Delphine Jones as she climbed out of her late model Toyota. "What he's doing is barely legal."

Fiona leaned against Celeste's Volkswagen which was parked next to Delphine's and studied the petite attorney. She wore a casual outfit consisting of an ankle length skirt in a rainbow of colors, an orange tee-shirt and a yellow blazer. Somehow the outfit worked on her and complimented her dark skin and cropped hair.

Fiona knew she had made the right decision in hiring Delphine, even though she was a bit unconventional. The attorney was a whirlwind of energy. She didn't waste any time, got things done quickly and, most importantly, she believed that Morgan was innocent.

"Shall we?" Fiona nodded her head toward the police station and Delphine started walking. Fiona, Celeste and Jolene followed.

"I'll go up and deal with Overton," Delphine said, "You can go visit your sister." Delphine looked at her watch. "She should be released within fifteen minutes. After that, I gotta run, so I'll get back in touch with you if I hear anything new. It's really just a waiting game after this. Overton *has* to come up with something concrete that ties Morgan to the murder scene before he can start to prosecute. Right now he's got nothing."

Fiona opened the police station door and motioned for Delphine to go in. The feisty attorney stormed up to the desk.

"I need to see Sheriff Overton, pronto," she barked at the desk clerk.

The clerk, a short, round woman whose head barely reached the top of the counter looked around nervously. "He's busy now."

Delphine slapped her hand on the counter. "I don't care what he's doing. You tell him if he doesn't talk to me now, the next time he sees me it will be on opposite sides of a wrongful arrest suit!"

The clerk's eyes went wide and she got up from her chair. "Yes, ma'am."

"And make sure somebody takes these girls down to see my client, Morgan Blackmoore." Delphine yelled after her, leaning over the counter.

Delphine turned and winked at Fiona as a uniformed officer came out from the back.

"This way, ladies," he gestured for them to file through the door he held open.

The girls were unusually silent as they followed the officer down a manila tiled corridor to a steel door that opened to reveal a set of concrete stairs.

They filed down the stairs, the echoe's of their footsteps sounding hollow, the musty smell getting stronger with each step. Fiona's heart lurched in her chest, thinking of poor Morgan in her barren, uncomfortable jail cell enduring this pungent mildew smell, and god only knew what else.

They trudged down a long corridor, toward a door made of metal bars which the officer pressed a button on the wall to open. He held it for the three girls. Fiona turned and her heart skipped when she noticed the looks on her sister's faces mirrored her own apprehensive feelings.

The room had three cells. The officer stopped in front of the last one and Fiona willed her feet to follow him. An iron fist squeezed her chest, she could barely breathe picturing what she would see when she looked in the cell—Morgan depressed and crying, curled on the cot all alone.

Then she heard a trill of laughter. Morgan's laughter. Her brow furrowed and she increased her pace.

"You have visitors, Morgan," The officer said into the cell and then stepped back to make room for Fiona, Celeste and Jolene to crowd around the front.

Fiona's mouth dropped open when she saw what was really going on in the cell. Morgan sat on the small bed, across from her in a chair sat Jake Cooper, a folding table in between them held what looked like the remnants of a pot roast meal complete with mashed potatoes and vegetables.

Morgan's face broke into a smile when she saw her sisters "Hey, you guys didn't have to all come down here." She got up and walked over to the bars.

"Morgan, what are you doing?" Fiona's eyes narrowed and she tilted her head toward the table of food and Jake.

Morgan looked back over her shoulder. "Oh, Jake just brought me supper, wasn't that nice of him?"

Fiona screwed up her face and scrutinized Jake as Morgan greeted her other sisters. *What was he up to?*

"I hope you didn't tell him anything." Fiona whispered to Morgan.

"Like what?" Morgan shrugged. "I don't have anything to tell."

In the background, Fiona could see Jake picking up what was left of their dinner. He stood and came toward them.

"Are these your sisters?" He asked.

"Yep, this is Celeste, Jolene and you already know Fiona, I think." Jake nodded to Fiona and shook hands with the others.

"Well, I think we can open the door and let them in to visit," he said nodding to the officer still standing behind them.

The door slid open and the girls rushed in to hug Morgan while Jake stepped out of the cell. Just then another officer appeared.

"Overton says to release her," he said to Jake.

"Well, looks like you're free to go." Jake nodded at Morgan, then stepped back to let the women procede him up the corridor.

"I can go?   You mean I'm cleared?" Morgan asked.

"No, you're still a suspect," the officer answered. "We just don't have enough to hold you."

"Oh." Morgan's face fell a little, but then she smiled. "Well, I know I'll be cleared soon enough so it's just as good."

They filed out, Morgan first and Fiona bringing up the rear. Jake stepped in line behind them. They retraced their steps up the corridor, up the stairs, then stopped at the desk to collect an envelope of Morgan's personal effects.

Fiona felt her heart swell at the look of joy on Morgan's face as they headed out the door that Jake held open for them. She cleared the doorway and Jake fell in behind her. She ignored the flip-flop of her stomach when he put his hand on the small of her back, attributing it to all the excitement and lack of dinner.

"Now, I expect you girls won't do anything silly," he said looking pointedly at Fiona.

She crossed her arms over her chest. "Like what?"

"Oh, you know, go poking around trying to figure out who the killer is?"

Fiona felt anger rising. Who was *he* to tell them what to do?

"Well, since the police seem hell bent on prosecuting my sister for it, I don't see we have much choice."

Jake looked down at the pavement and pushed a pebble around with his shoe. When he looked back up, Fiona's heart lurched at something she saw in his eyes. Concern?

Fear? She wasn't sure which, but his next words chilled her.

"Look, I think we might be dealing with someone very dangerous here. You girls should stay out of it. Let the police handle it."

Fiona snickered, but Morgan cut her off before she could say anything.

"Of course we will, won't we Fi?" Fiona noticed the way Morgan raised her eyebrow at her and took that as a warning to keep quiet.

"Sure." She managed to choke the words out.

"Good, then I'll wish you good luck and send you on your way." He nodded at them, turned and strode back into the police station.

Fiona stared at his retreating back. She had no intention of following his orders, especially when it seemed like the police were content to pin the murder on Morgan. She didn't feel confident that they would conduct a thorough investigation to find the real killer. For all she knew the dangerous person she needed to be afraid of was Jake Cooper, himself.

Chapter Seven

Morgan curled her feet under her in the oversized chair and took a sip of chamomile tea. Reaching down, she stroked the silky fur of Belladonna who lay on her lap contentedly purring. It felt good to be home.

Morgan felt safe here in her favorite room with her sisters. It wasn't the largest one in their twenty four room home, but it was the most comfortable. Decorated in grays and blues, Morgan could see her mother's touch everywhere; from the overstuffed white furniture, to the giant starfish and seashells on the mantle, to the chipped paint coffee table. The room sat on the east side of the house and the large bay window offered an unobstructed view of the Atlantic Ocean a mere two hundred feet away.

"I feel awful that you guys had to pawn that necklace ... I didn't even know there was stuff like that up there," Morgan said, glancing upwards toward the attic.

"We didn't have much choice. It didn't look like they were going to let you out,"

Fiona said. "Unless you were planning on charming Jake Cooper into springing you."

Morgan laughed, "Hardly." Then she narrowed her eyes at Fiona "He's not the enemy, you know."

Fiona snorted. "He's the one that cuffed you and put you in the back of the police car!"

"Only because he was ordered to."

Fiona glared at Morgan. "Think what you want, but I'm warning you, you'd better watch out around him. I sense that he's trouble."

Morgan cocked an eyebrow at her sister, wondering why Fiona was protesting so much about Jake. She didn't think Jake was trouble. She thought Jake could be a valuable ally. And he seemed like a perfect match for Fiona. Morgan could practically see the sparks fly between them. She was certain Jake felt the same way ... she'd noticed how his gaze lingered on Fiona at the jail. If only Fiona would just wake up and notice it herself. Maybe she would have to give her a special herbal tea to help things along.

"I didn't want to take the necklace," Cal said coming in from the kitchen with two glasses full of green juice. "I could just lend you guys the money."

Morgan watched Cal hand Celeste one of the glasses and then sit next to her on the couch. He'd been sitting on their front porch when they returned home, worried about her. Cal was the closest thing they had to a brother and she would never risk their relationship by borrowing money from him.

"Don't be silly, we would never take advantage of you like that," Fiona said, echoing Morgan's thoughts.

Cal made a face. "Oh for crying out loud, I have the money. Besides, that necklace is a family heirloom, and a nice one at that. You girls should really get up in the attic and see what else is there."

"What kind of stuff *was* up there, Fi?" Morgan asked.

"Just a bunch of old junk, furniture, dishes, boxes packed full of god knows what." Fiona furrowed her brow. "There was one interesting thing, though."

Celeste and Cal both raised their eyebrows.

"What?" they said at the same time, then fell back on the couch laughing and punched each other lightly in the arm.

"It was an old book. It looked ancient, but I couldn't find any date; a handwritten journal of some sort."

"What did it say?"

"I don't know, I couldn't make out the writing and I didn't have much time to study it."

"Maybe we *should* go up there and look around." Morgan said. Belladonna let out a loud meow and hopped down from her lap. Morgan watched her walk toward the kitchen, tail swishing high in the air.

Just as the cat reached the kitchen doorway, she turned and looked right at Morgan as if to say "Come on. What are you waiting for?" Morgan laughed to herself at her own overactive imagination. The cat wasn't trying to communicate with her. That was ridiculous ... wasn't it?

Jolene's eyes went wide. "I don't think we should, Mom told us not to."

Mom didn't know we'd be scrambling to come up with tax money or trying to avoid getting charged with murder.

Cal leaned back on the couch, stretching out his long legs. "Well, it's up to you guys, but if you need my help in figuring out what anything is worth, let me know."

Morgan studied Cal from the other side of the room. She knew his intent was honest, he really did want to help and he did have a lot of knowledge about antiques since he'd been running his family pawn shop for almost a decade. She knew they could trust him and she filed the information away for later in case they got desperate for money.

Cal was about the nicest guy she knew. Tall, dark and handsome, he was also the most eligible bachelor in town. It was rumored that women pawned jewelry at his shop just to talk to him, hoping for a date. Morgan didn't know how true that was, but he sure would be a good catch for the right women. Morgan herself might have been interested, but there was only one man she would ever love and he'd left town ... and her ... years ago.

"Okay, so what do we do now?" Celeste interrupted Morgan's thoughts.

"About what?" Jolene asked.

"We have to do something to help prove Morgan didn't kill Prudence Littlefield."

"I don't know how much we really need to do. Don't you guys think the police will find the real killer?" Morgan asked.

"Pffft." Fiona waved her hand in the air. "I don't know about you guys, but I'm not going to sit back while the police bumble their way through an investigation. There's a killer out there and I don't care what Jake Copper says, I'm going to find out who it is."

She glanced around the room piercing each of them with her steely blue gaze.

"Now, who's with me?"

Chapter Eight

Fiona woke up the next morning in a tangle of sheets. The questions running around in her head had kept her awake all night. Who could have killed Prudence? Why? What should they do to find the killer?

She swung her legs over the bed and looked out the window. Squinting, she brought her hand up to shade her eyes from the glare of the morning sun reflecting off the water. It was just shortly after sunrise and looked like it was going to be a beautiful day. But somehow, Fiona wasn't enthusiastic about getting out of bed.

Coffee ... she needed coffee.

She stood up and stretched, wincing at the cracking sound coming from her back. Throwing a sweatshirt on over the tee-shirt and sweatpants she wore to bed, she wrapped her long red curls in a ponytail and headed down to the kitchen.

The front stairs creaked as she walked down them, echoing eerily throughout the silent house. *Was everyone else still asleep?*

They had stayed up late the night before, hashing out a plan of action. Whoever had killed Prudence must have been in the coffee shop when she had her run in with Morgan, or at least heard about it from someone who was there. Fiona and Morgan would try to find out who was in the coffee shop that morning. Celeste's job was to find out if any of her customers at the yoga center knew anything and Cal was going to ask some of his seedier clients at the pawn shop what they knew about it. Fiona didn't want Jolene getting involved, but Jolene had insisted on asking around to see if any of her friends had heard anything about the murder.

Fiona padded into the kitchen, feeling the cold of the granite tile on her bare feet. She made her way to the coffee maker and popped in a k-cup. She really needed a large latte to get her going, but this would have to do until she could make it to the coffee shop.

"Meow." Belladonna jabbed at her calf, the needle-like claws raking her flesh.

"Ouch! Cut that out." Fiona swatted at the cat with her foot.

Belladonna responded by trotting over to the kitchen door and scratching at it. "Meow!"

"Oh, you want me to let you out. Why didn't you just say so?" Fiona took her cup of steaming coffee and walked over to the door. Peeking out the window, she could see the sunlight hitting the tiny plants in Morgan's herb garden.

She opened the door and Belladonna streaked out into the garden. Fiona followed relishing the feel of the dew soaked grass on her bare feet, even if it was a little cold.

She turned her face to the sun and closed her eyes, inhaling the bitter aroma of the coffee.

"Meooooow."

Fiona opened her eyes and looked toward the cat who was scratching at the ground.

"Belladonna, stop that! Morgan will be mad if you dig up her plants."

Belladonna didn't stop. She dug even more furiously at the ground. Fiona's brows knit together as she watched the cat. She was digging in an isolated part of the garden ... one Morgan hadn't planted in yet.

"I hope you aren't digging up a dead mouse."

Fiona walked over. Looking down at the patch of dirt Belladonna was working on, she saw something strange. She bent down for a closer look.

"What's this?" She tugged at the bright orange fabric.

Her heart froze when she recognized the sunflower scarf in her hands.

Prudence Littlefield's scarf. The one she was wearing the day she was murdered.

Fiona couldn't help but wonder, what was it doing in Morgan's garden?

Chapter Nine

"If you ask me, it was Berta Crumm who done it."

Fiona narrowed her eyes at Agatha Beesley who stood on the other side of her jewelry case, trying a carnelian bracelet on her wrist.

"What do you mean?"

"Well, Berta and Prudence had a long going feud," she said twisting her ample wrist to study the bracelet from different angles.

Who didn't Prudence have a feud with?

Agatha glanced around the shop then leaned in toward Fiona, lowering her voice. "Prudence stole Ed away from Berta, you know."

Fiona made a face. Picturing a love triangle between Prudence, Ed and Berta, even in their younger days was too much. She gulped down the rest of her latte wishing the cup held something stronger.

"So, you think Berta might have killed Prudence because she stole Ed form her fifty some-odd years ago? It hardly seems likely she would have waited that long."

Agatha nodded, returning her attention to the bracelet. "They've had quite a few fights about it over the years, maybe the opportunity just presented itself."

Fiona looked across the shop at Morgan who was busy preparing a salve of ground up jewelweed to help someone with a bad case of poison ivy. She'd arrived late at the shop after getting their tea and coffee from the cafe and hadn't told Morgan about the scarf, yet. Her stomach churned just thinking about it. She was afraid of what Morgan might say about the scarf being buried in the garden. *Did she bury it there, and, if so, why?*

"I'll take this and those matching earrings." Agatha interrupted her thoughts.

Fiona packaged up the jewelry and rang up the sale, thanking Agatha for her purchase and her information.

The bell over the door announced Agatha's departure and Morgan looked up, meeting Fiona's eyes.

"We should at least talk to Berta," she said.

Fiona nodded. "And figure out anyone else who might have wanted her dead. She was mean to almost everyone, maybe there are other people who would have wanted to kill her."

"Maybe she ran into someone in the woods, was her usual nasty self, and they killed her in a fit of anger."

"We should probably talk to her husband too," Fiona said. "The spouse is the first person they usually question in the movies. And we need to come up with a list of everyone who witnessed your conversation in the cafe that morning."

Morgan sighed. "Jeez, almost half the town was there." She closed her eyes and chewed on her bottom lip. "I remember seeing Elle from the bakery, Katie Morton, Sandy Shawnee, Eli Stark..." Her voice trailed off. "It's no use. We could never talk to all these people. How will we narrow it down?"

Fiona felt her stomach sinking. Morgan was right. Too many people had been in the cafe. Not to mention that word had probably spread all around town about their altercation. Anyone could have known what Morgan had said to Prudence that day.

They sat in silence, each of them wrestling with their own thoughts. The grandfather clock, passed down by some distant relative, tick-tocked off the seconds measuring the passage of time. *Time.*

"That's it!" Fiona snapped her fingers.

Morgan raised her eyebrows. "What?"

"Maybe instead of trying to prove who *did* do it, we can prove that you *couldn't* have done it." Fiona held her breath waiting to see Morgan's reaction. She *did* feel sure her sister couldn't have killed Prudence despite the incriminating scarf in her garden, didn't she?

"How would we do *that*?" Morgan narrowed her eyes, tilting her head to one side.

"Easy. You came here straight after you left the coffee shop, right?"

Morgan nodded.

"Then all we need to do is establish a timeline and prove that you didn't have time to kill Prudence."

"But we don't even know exactly what time she was killed ... maybe we can get that information from Jake," Fiona ignored the mischievous glint in Morgan's eyes and pursed her lips.

"No, we can't trust him. But we *can* trust Delphine, I'll see if I can get the time of death from her. But we do know she was strangled in the woods in between the coffee shop and her house."

"Which is only about one quarter mile from here."

"How fast can you run a quarter mile?"

"Run? You know I never run." Morgan laughed.

"Well, if you just strangled someone, you might be running."

Morgan shrugged. "I don't know. Five minutes maybe?"

"But you'd have to go out of your way to get to the woods. We need to find out exactly *where* Prudence was killed. Visit the scene of the crime, so to speak. Then we can figure out how long it would take you to go from the cafe, to the scene, strangle her and then come here."

"How long do you think it takes to strangle someone?" Morgan asked.

"I have no idea, but if we can prove that you wouldn't have had time, they'll have to drop the charges."

"Yes, but I still don't see how we can *prove* it."

"Well, I remember looking at my watch when you came in because I was dying for my latte. It was just after ten past eight. Maybe someone who was in the coffee shop will remember what time you left?"

Morgan looked at her dubiously. "Do you really think so?"

Fiona sighed. It *was* a long shot, they needed something more concrete.

"Wait a minute ... did you get a receipt?"

"Probably, I usually just stuff them in my jeans and then take them out and toss them on laundry day." Morgan's face brightened. "Hey it might still be in here!"

Fiona watched Morgan dig in her pockets, a cloud passing over her face as she came up empty.

"I was wearing these yesterday. They took everything out of the pockets at the jail, so, if I have one, it must be in the envelope they gave me."

"We'll look for that tonight. It might be a great way to prove you are innocent. If the police will believe me when I tell them what time you got here ..."

Morgan nodded. "Yeah, seems like Overton might not go for that. But it's worth a try."

"Okay, well anyway back to—"

Fiona was interrupted by the trilling of her cell phone on the workbench behind her. She turned to look at the display and her heart lurched. Jolene. She never called her at work unless something was wrong.

She dived for the phone. "Hello?"

"Fiona? It's Jolene. You guys better get home quick. The police are here and they're digging up the yard!"

Chapter Ten

Skidding her truck to a stop at the edge of the driveway, Fiona jumped out, her heart pounding in her chest as she ran to the garden on the East side of the house.

Her body tensed with anger when she saw what was going on. Sheriff Overton stood watch over Jake Cooper and another officer while they turned the earth over with shovels. She noticed they were in the exact area where she had found the scarf. *How did they know exactly where to look?*

Jolene stood off to the side, her eyes wide. Morgan ran to her and put a comforting arm around her.

Fiona stood frozen, staring at the men, trying to get her mouth to work when the screech of tires in the driveway caught her attention. She turned her head in time to see Delphine running toward Overton flapping her arms.

"Just *what* do you think you are doing?" she demanded.

Fiona felt her stomach roil with anger at the smug look on Overton's face. He stared Delphine down, his tongue switching the toothpick from side to side.

"We got an anonymous tip that someone saw your client bury a crucial piece of evidence here."

"What are you talking about?" Delphine turned to Morgan. "Do you know anything about this?"

Morgan shook her head.

Fiona noticed the perplexed look on Morgan's face. Either she'd taken acting lessons, or she really did know nothing about the scarf.

"Let me see the warrant." Delphine stuck her hand out toward Overton.

"Listen Missy, I don't need a warrant. I got a tip."

"You most certainly do need one," Delphine countered. "And I suggest you either produce one or get off my client's property unless you want a lawsuit. And don't call me Missy!"

Fiona noticed Jake carefully putting the dirt back, taking care not to disturb Morgan's tender seedlings. He looked up and she felt a jolt go through her when their eyes met.

Overton looked down at Delphine then glared over at Morgan. "If we have to take time to get a warrant, that will give your client a chance to move the evidence."

"Well, you should have thought of that before and gone through the proper channels." Delphine spit back at him. "Now move it."

Overton nodded to Jake and the other officer who was leaning on his shovel listening to the exchange.

"Let's pack it up boys, we'll come back later. I know the evidence is here." He stared at Morgan as he said the words then started off toward the front of the house. Fiona shrank back when he brushed past her.

Delphine turned to Fiona. "Do you know what he's talking about?"

Fiona's stomach flipped. *Should she tell her?* Her first instinct was to keep quiet. If

79

she let Delphine know she'd found the scarf, she'd probably make her give it up to the police, and Fiona had a sneaking suspicion the police were planning to use that scarf to incriminate Morgan.

"No idea," she said, mentally crossing her fingers.

"Let me know if he comes here again without a warrant."

"Okay, thanks for getting here so fast." Fiona had called the lawyer as soon as she'd hung up with Jolene. Delphine must have had to break some speeding records to get there when she did.

"All in a day's work," Delphine said, nodding to Fiona, then turning and trotting off toward her car.

Fiona could see Jolene almost in tears over by the house.

"I didn't know the right thing to do," she was saying to Morgan.

"You called us right away, that was the right thing," Morgan assured her, then ushered her into the house by the kitchen door.

Fiona started over toward the door herself, noticing that Jake was still in the garden, apparently trying to put it back the way he found it.

She stomped over, wanting him off the property along with the other members of the police.

"You can go now too, we'll take care of this." She stood with her hands on her hips.

Jake glanced around then leaned toward her. "Listen, I think something funny is going on. This tip ... it just didn't seem right."

Fiona stepped back, narrowing her eyes. *Was this some sort of trick?*

"What do you mean?"

"There's a certain procedure, but this one ... it just seemed to come out of thin air."

He had stepped even closer now so that he towered over her. She could smell the spicy scent of his aftershave. His gray eyes mesmerized her and she stepped closer. He put his hand on her arm, causing a cascade of tingles to flutter in her lower belly. He leaned closer toward her.

"You better warn Morgan to be on her guard. Something isn't right here."

Fiona blinked at his warning. Then he let her arm go abruptly, turned and walked toward the front of the house.

She stared after him, noticing how his backside filled out his uniform just perfectly. Then she shook herself.

What was she thinking?

Even though Jake's warning seemed sincere, she still didn't think she could trust him. His concern for Morgan made her feel a little funny. If she didn't know better, she'd swear it was jealousy. Laughing at herself, she turned toward the kitchen door.

That was ridiculous ... she didn't give two figs about Jake Cooper. Why would she feel jealous if he had the hots for Morgan?

Chapter Eleven

Fiona came in the kitchen door just as Celeste came in the front door.

"We're in here!" Morgan called out into the front hallway.

Celeste came rushing in, her face flushed. "What happened, I heard the police were here?"

Morgan got up to make tea while Fiona told Celeste about the police digging in the garden. She paced the room, hands flying in the air, anger rising inside her as she relayed the events.

When she was done, Morgan handed her a cup of tea.

"What's this? I don't drink that stuff, I drink coffee." Fiona pushed the cup away.

"Right now you need something calming, not caffeine to ramp you up more, just sit and drink it." Morgan pushed the cup into her hands and pulled out a chair which Fiona obediently sat in.

She took a sip and almost spit it out. "Blech. This tastes like grass, what's in here?"

"Oh a little chamomile and some other herbs to relax you. Drink," Morgan commanded, leaning against the kitchen counter on the other side of the bar.

Fiona wrinkled her nose, but took another sip. Okay, maybe it wasn't so bad. And she did feel calmer already.

"I don't think I understand. What did they think was in the garden?" Celeste asked.

"I'm not sure, some sort of evidence," Morgan answered. "Fi, do you know what that was all about?"

Fiona's heart tightened in her chest. She had to come clean with her sisters.

"Well, actually I do," she said. Setting down her cup, she looked at Morgan, her stomach fluttering. She hoped her sister wouldn't be mad that she didn't come to her right away.

"Well?" Morgan lifted her shoulders, "What is it?"

"There *was* some evidence in the garden, except I found it before they did."

Celeste gasped, "What was it?"

"Prudence Littlefield's scarf. The one she was wearing the day she was killed."

Morgan, Celeste and Jolene stared at her in silence.

"What are you talking about?" Morgan asked.

"This morning, I was the first one up. Belladonna wanted to go out, so I let her out the door here, next to the garden. It was a beautiful morning and I went out for a breath of fresh air. That's when I found the scarf. It was buried on the edge of the garden, near the tomato seedlings."

"Buried? Then how did you find it?" Jolene asked.

"Well, it actually wasn't me who found it. It was Belladonna. She led me right to it."

Everyone turned to look at Belladonna who lay sleeping on the wide windowsill at the back of the kitchen. She turned her head toward them, opened one sleepy blue eye, then closed it and went back to sleep.

"She was digging in the garden and dug it right up," Fiona added.

Morgan looked away from the cat and Fiona flinched at the anger she saw in her sister's eyes.

"So, you had the scarf and didn't even tell me? We were at work together all morning and you never mentioned it. Why?"

Fiona's heart squeezed. She didn't want Morgan to know she had doubted her.

"I didn't really get a chance," she said, mostly telling the truth. "There was someone in the shop when I got there with the coffee and then Agatha came in, then we got involved in talking about how to find the killer and then Jolene called."

Morgan nodded, looking away. "Where is it now?"

"I hid it in my room," Fiona said, picturing the scarf tucked neatly in her secret hiding place under a floor board in the corner.

"Shouldn't we bring it to the police?" Celeste asked.

"No!" Fiona, Morgan, and Jolene all shouted at once.

"They'll probably just use it against Morgan," Fiona said. "Someone clearly planted the scarf there. It could be someone with ties to the police, or maybe it isn't, but one thing is clear ... someone is out to frame Morgan.

Morgan sighed. "Okay, well since we are all here, let's use this time for something productive. Celeste, did you find anything out at the yoga studio?"

"I talked to a few people that were in the coffee shop. Pretty much everyone thought it was funny—what you said to Prudence. Of course, no one thinks you killed her. But I didn't hear any clues or anything."

"I haven't talked to everyone in my circle yet," Jolene said, "But I did see something strange on Facebook."

"Oh, what?" Morgan asked.

"Josh Gray made some strange posts that made it look like he was going to invest in something expensive ... which was odd, since he doesn't have any money."

Fiona wrinkled her brow. "What would that have to do with Prudence's murder?"

"Probably nothing; Josh is a thug, and he brags a lot. He might just be blowing steam, or maybe he did a big drug deal." Jolene shrugged. "Probably nothing to do with the murder, but it was out of the ordinary."

"Has anyone talked to Cal?" Fiona asked.

"I did," Morgan said. "He hadn't heard anything."

Fiona chewed the inside of her cheek. She didn't know where to start to try to figure out who the killer was. Then she remembered, they might not have to find the killer at all.

"Hey, what about the receipt from the coffee shop that morning, did you look in the envelope?"

Morgan's eyebrows shot up. "No, I forgot all about that." She spun around and grabbed the envelope from the counter behind her. Opening it, she dumped the contents on the island.

All four girls leaned over to examine the pile.

Chapstick, a five dollar bill, some change, a couple of business cards and her shoe laces. No receipt.

"It's not there," Morgan said, her face crumbling.

"Are you sure you even had one?" Fiona asked. "I usually just toss mine in the barrel."

"I'm pretty sure. Usually I just shove them in my pocket with the change if I have to juggle two cups like I did that morning. But I can't be certain."

The four girls bent down to examine the pile again and then looked up at each other.

Fiona noticed the grim look on Morgan's face as she said, "If I did have that receipt, then someone at the police station took it. I have to admit, it really does look like someone is trying to frame me for killing Prudence."

Celeste's brow knit together. "It does seem that way, but why?"

"I don't know," Morgan said. "But these latest developments call for some drastic action and I think I know just the person to help us."

Chapter Twelve

Jake stared at the Littlefield file on his desk. He'd been flipping through it for an hour looking for inconsistencies, but nothing stuck out at him.

Why was Overton so steamed about not finding that scarf?

Back in Boston, Jake had followed up on his share of anonymous tips. Most of them turned out to be a dead end. Surely, Overton knew this? It just didn't make sense that he would be so mad at not finding the *supposed* murder weapon. Unless he *knew* without a reasonable doubt that it would be there.

And how could he know that?

The only way Jake could figure he would know for sure was if it had been planted on his orders ... or by someone he trusted explicitly.

What he couldn't figure out was why. It didn't make any sense to frame Morgan for Prudence's death. He supposed it could just be convenient. Knowing about the argument they'd had in the coffee shop, the killer could have used the newt to cast suspicion on Morgan. Maybe they took the scarf for added insurance.

But then, that begged the question, why would someone kill Prudence?

Jake knew the logical thing would be to find out who stood to benefit from her murder, but Overton wasn't doing that, he seemed content to pin it on Morgan.

Jake was sure there was something else going on, and he'd be willing to bet that Overton was right in the middle of it.

He let out a sigh and snapped the file closed. All the file really told him was that Littlefield had been strangled and the murder weapon, presumed to be this scarf Overton was so hot to dig up, was not found at the scene. ... which would lead one to believe the murderer had it. But why would the murderer take it?

His thoughts turned to the Blackmoore girls. He felt certain the redhead, Fiona, was going to be even more determined to find the real killer now. He could hardly blame her. His heart clenched when he thought of how alone the girls must feel. To them, it must seem like everyone is against them.

But they wouldn't be alone, because Jake had already made up his mind to help find the real killer and it had nothing to do with the silky way Fiona's skin felt under his hand, or the way he couldn't get the smell of her strawberry shampoo out of his mind. It was ingrained in him to find the truth, to serve justice. That was why he had become a cop. And he'd been a pretty good detective in Boston ... before the accident.

Jake got up from his chair. He'd have to do his detecting in his spare time, if Overton caught on to his extracurricular activities it could cost him his job, so he'd have to be very careful. But he knew just where to start.

Overton had rushed them through the crime scene the day of the murder. At the time he didn't think anything of it, but now, he felt like he should go back over it with a fine tooth comb. He was sure there must be a clue there that they had overlooked before; a clue that would, hopefully, lead them to the real killer.

Chapter Thirteen

Fiona pressed the doorbell glancing over at Morgan. It was early afternoon and the sun had heated the day to a pleasant seventy-five degrees. Fiona looked around the tidy porch already dotted with flowering plants and listened to the chirp of birds.

A sound at the door caught her attention and she looked back in time to see Berta's face poke through the opening.

"Oh, it's you girls," she said swinging the door wide. "Do come in."

Fiona stepped back and let Morgan enter first.

"I put together some herbal teas for you," Morgan said, handing a small basket to Berta.

Berta lifted the cloth that was on top and peered in. "Oh, wonderful! Let's go in the kitchen and I'll fix us some tea. I have ginger cookies fresh out of the oven."

Fiona furrowed her brow. Ginger cookies? Killers didn't bake cookies and invite you in for tea, did they?

Fiona followed them into the tiny kitchen which looked like something out of the 1950s. Yellow gingham curtains fluttered on either side of an open window. A small round cornered fridge sat at one end and a tiny white stove sat next to it. Wooden cabinets painted a cheery yellow brightened the small room. The smell of ginger hung in the air.

Berta motioned for them to sit at a yellow Formica table while she busied herself putting on the teapot and selecting some tea from the basket.

Her selection made, she turned to Morgan. "I hope that nasty business with Prudence isn't affecting you too much, dear."

Morgan shrugged. "Well, it is a little unsettling."

Berta leaned in toward her "Did you kill her?" She asked with a gleam in her eye.

Morgan gasped. Her eyebrows shot up. "What? No, I didn't kill her."

Berta looked disappointed. "Oh. Well, no one would blame you if you did. I might even thank you."

"That's one reason why we are here. Do you know who might have wanted Prudence dead?" Fiona asked.

Berta looked up at the ceiling. "There are so many people that hated her, but if I had to pick one person—"

Fiona perched on the edge of her seat waiting for the name when Berta was interrupted by the whistle of the kettle. The older woman turned to grabbed it from the stove. Fiona notice she grabbed it awkwardly with her left hand while she kept her right hand next to her body.

Morgan must have noticed too because she shot up out of her chair. "Let me help you with that. Did you hurt your arm?"

"Thank you, dear. Yes, I sprained my wrist." She said wincing and pulling her arm in closer as she handed Morgan the teapot.

Fiona and Morgan glanced at each other.

"When did that happen?" Fiona asked taking a ginger cookie from the plate Berta had put on the table.

Berta wrinkled her brow. "Oh, sometime last week," she said absentmindedly waving her good arm.

Fiona took a bite of her cookie, the combination of sugar and spice tingled on her taste buds.

"You were saying ..." she prompted hoping to get Berta to spill out the name of the one person she thought might have killed Prudence.

Berta furrowed her brow. "What, dear?"

Fiona sighed. "Before you poured the tea, you were saying if you had to pick one person who might have killed Prudence ..."

"Oh, right. Well, that would be Josiah Littlefield, of course. Ed's brother."

Fiona raised an eyebrow over her steaming mug. "His brother?"

"Yes, Josiah hated Prudence from the start. She was so controlling, demanding. He hated that she wouldn't let Ed do anything. And she controlled the money with an iron fist," Berta said. Then her forehead creased into a frown. "That's why it was so strange that her and Ed were fighting about selling their property to Eli Stark. She didn't want to sell and he did. I would have thought she would have wanted the money."

"They were fighting?" Morgan asked.

"Yes ... well, nothing unusual." Berta narrowed her eyes. "If you're thinking Ed might have killed her I can assure you he did not. That man is gentle as a lamb. He wouldn't hurt a flea."

The wistful look on Berta's face made Fiona's heart soften. She sipped her tea and studied the older woman. It must be heart wrenching to love someone that belonged to another all this time.

"Have you seen Ed?" Berta asked, breaking into Fiona's thoughts. "Is he okay? I haven't seen him in years ... not since the restraining order, but now that Prudence is gone, maybe ..."

"Restraining order?"

Berta waved her arms. "Oh it was silly, Prudy took it out on me years ago saying I threatened her, but I think she just didn't want me near Ed. She was jealous of me, you know."

Fiona and Morgan exchanged another glance. *Could Berta have killed Prudence?* Apparently she'd already threatened her.

"Were you at home that morning?" Fiona asked.

Berta looked at her blankly, the said. "Oh, you mean when Prudence was killed? I believe I was at the dentist. Oh ... wait ... that was Tuesday, right? That's the day I get my hair done. Why do you ask?"

"Just wondering if you saw anything, or heard anything."

"Oh. No. Well I'm pretty far off the beaten path here," Berta answered.

"Is there anyone else you can think of who might have killed Prudence?" Morgan asked.

Berta pursed her lips and then shook her head. "I really don't know. I hate to say it, but whoever killed her did us all a favor."

Fiona wiped the cookie crumbs from her lips and stood up. "Thanks for the tea and cookies. Can we help you clean up?"

"Oh no, dear, you girls run along. Thank you for bringing me these lovely teas." She indicated the basket Morgan had given her.

Berta ushered them out through the living room and onto the porch, waving goodbye with her good arm before she shut the door.

Fiona turned to Morgan on the way to the car.

"Do you think she did it?"

Morgan glanced back at the house. "That nice old lady? Would she even have the strength?"

"Fifty years of pent up hatred might give her the strength. And her wrist? What if she injured it in the struggle with Prudence?"

Morgan chewed her bottom lip. "She could have, but she said it was sprained last week. Before the murder. We need to check with Doc Brundage and see if we can verify that and we should also make sure she really was getting her hair done that morning."

"I don't feel like we are any closer to figuring out who killed Prudence. In fact, it sounds like Berta, Josiah and maybe even Ed would have had a motive."

Morgan opened the passenger door to the truck and turned to look at Fiona as she crossed in front of it to the driver's side. "Yeah, it does. Maybe all three of them teamed up and did it together."

Fiona raised her brows as she swung herself up into the driver's seat. "I guess there's only one way to find out. Interview the others and see who has an alibi for that morning."

Chapter Fourteen

Fiona pulled up in front of *Sticks and Stones* and cut the engine in her truck. The mid-afternoon sun filtered through the trees creating a fairy-tale like atmosphere. She leaned back in her seat listening to the bees buzzing and birds chirping while she admired the azaleas in full bloom on either side of the cottage.

A stone pathway led up to the porch in front where Morgan had put out several rocking chairs. One of which, she noticed with a start, was rocking on its own. No, not on its own ... Belladonna lay curled on the seat, her white fur almost blending with the white wicker of the chair.

"Did you leave Belladonna out this morning?" she asked Morgan.

"No, you know I always lock her inside, why?"

Fiona pointed and Morgan followed the direction of her finger, her eyes widening when she noticed the cat.

"How, the heck did she get here?"

Fiona shrugged, opening her door. "I thought I'd seen her darting around town before, I have no idea how she gets out. Maybe Jolene lets her out."

"Or maybe she has some secret escape route through the basement," Morgan mused, as the girls slid out of the truck.

"One we didn't find as kids?" Fiona's lips turned up in a smile as she remembered the fun they used to have as kids exploring the nooks and crannies of the giant basement in their old home. They had always fantasized about secret tunnels that led to the ocean, but, of course they never found any.

A memory tugged at the corner of her mind, one that did involve secret tunnels and caverns in the cliffs under her home—just a silly childhood fantasy she figured, even though the memory did seem very real, if a bit fuzzy.

"Meow." Belladonna hopped down from the chair and wound her way in between Morgan's legs.

"Don't try to get in my good graces. You're a bad kitty for straying so far from home. You could get hurt." Morgan bent to pick the cat up while Fiona unlocked the door to their shop.

Once inside Morgan gave Belladonna a kiss on the forehead, then the cat squirmed away, jumping down to the floor where she proceeded to slink her way around the shop, sniffing and exploring while Morgan and Fiona got to work.

The rest of the afternoon, was a whirlwind of activity. Fiona had worried that Morgan's arrest would be bad for business but, in fact, the opposite was true. It seemed everyone in the area wanted to stop in and get an herbal remedy, tea or buy some crystals or jewelry as an excuse to talk about the murder.

Morgan mixed up herbal remedies to treat seasickness, insect bites, arthritis pain and flatulence. Fiona sold several crystal spheres, two of her best geodes and three pairs of earrings.

Belladonna lounged on top of the bookshelf by the door where Morgan kept her books on herbs, stretched out along the top with her tail curled over the edge as if she didn't have a care in the world.

By five-thirty, both girls were exhausted and ready to close up for the day. Fiona was doing one last adjustment to her jewelry display which meant she was bent over the case, her backside high in the air when the bell above the door chimed.

"My, my, what an outstanding view."

Fiona's heart jerked and she whirled around at the sound of the raspy voice. Eli Stark stood in the doorway, his beady black eyes still staring at the spot where her backside had been just seconds before.

"What do you want?" Morgan narrowed her eyes at him.

Belladonna took one look at him, arched her back and hissed from the top of the bookshelf, causing Stark to jerk sideways.

"What's that?"

Morgan laughed. "It's our cat. Seems like she doesn't like you."

Stark gave Belladonna a long glare then turned his attention back to Morgan.

"I just came by to see if you ladies had changed your mind about selling this property. I figured you might need money with your new lawyer bills and all," he smirked.

Morgan tilted her chin in the air. "We have no intention of selling, right, Fi?"

Stark turned his leering gaze on Fiona who straightened up in front of the case. "That's right, and if we were going to sell, it certainly wouldn't be to you!"

Stark walked toward Fiona, stopping a mere inch from where she stood. She backed up a step, bumping into the display case which prevented her from getting further away. Stark leaned in to her, his greasy black hair dangling down beside his face.

"Well, I hope you girls change your mind, I'd hate to see you struggle for money in order to get your sister's name cleared."

Fiona's stomach dropped when he reached out to touch a lock of her hair. She slapped his hand away, shrinking back. "Get out!"

Suddenly, someone grabbed Stark from behind and spun him around. Fiona's eyes widened in surprise when she saw Jake Cooper standing there looking down at Stark.

"You heard the lady," Jake said, pointing to the door. "Get out."

Stark straightened his back and sidestepped away from Jake making his way to the door. He paused at it and turned "If you ladies change your minds, you know where to find me."

He opened the door, but before he could escape, Belladonna hissed and batted him with her claws. Stark swatted at her, but she was too quick for him. He turned back to glare at Fiona then disappeared through the door.

"What was *that* all about?" Jake swiveled his head looking first at Fiona then at Morgan.

Fiona let out a long breath. "That's Eli Stark, a real estate developer. He's been after us to sell this piece of land so he can build condos or something."

"Thanks for scaring him off." Morgan said to Jake.

"We could have taken care of him ourselves," Fiona crossed her arms against her chest. "What can we help *you* with?"

Jake raised his eyebrows and looked back at Morgan. Fiona noticed that he wasn't wearing his cop uniform. Which hopefully meant he wasn't there on police business. But then, why *was* he there?

She let her eyes wander over the plain gray tee-shirt he wore and noticed uncomfortably that the shirt accentuated his broad shoulders and extra-large biceps, making her wonder what was under the rest of it.

Her gaze seemed to have a mind of its own and made its way down to his trim waist. He was wearing faded jeans and Fiona felt her cheeks grow hot when she started to imagine what was under them.

"I asked him to come here. Jake's going to help us." Morgan's words caused Fiona to rip her gaze from Jake and focus it on her sister.

"What? Why?" she sputtered.

"I thought we needed some help finding the killer," Morgan said.

Fiona narrowed her eyes. "I don't think we can trust anyone but ourselves to do that."

"Look, it's clear that Overton wants to pin this on me. I have no idea why, but I'm pretty sure having someone on the inside can't hurt."

Fiona nodded her head toward Jake. "But *he* could be feeding everything you tell him *to* Overton."

Morgan looked over at Jake who stood quietly in the middle of the room swiveling his head back and forth as if at a tennis match while he watched the two sisters battle it out. Fiona noticed Belladonna had wandered over to make his acquaintance which consisted of weaving in and out between his ankles.

"I don't think so. My gut instincts tell me we can trust him. Besides Jake has plenty of detective experience from his last job. He could be an invaluable asset."

Fiona felt butterflies in her stomach. The trouble was she couldn't be sure if it was trepidation at letting Jake help them or the fact that she kept noticing that he looked pretty good out of his cop clothes.

Finally, she took a deep breath and let it out. "Ok, fine. It's your ass on the line." She waved a hand in the air.

"Great. Now that we have that settled, let's talk about what we plan to do." Jake said, bending down to pet Belladonna who mewed appreciatively.

Fiona finished putting her tools away and flipped the sign on the shop door to "closed" while Morgan told Jake about their visit to Berta Crumm.

Jake leaned against the counter in front of Morgan. Fiona could tell he was listening intently. Maybe he *would* be helpful. Morgan's gut instincts about people were usually right, but Fiona couldn't help but feel a little nervous about letting a stranger try to help with something so important.

"Those sound like good leads to follow up on," Jake said. "I can check with the hospital to see when Berta was treated for that sprain."

"I also think we need to go look at the place where Prudence was killed," Morgan said.

"I was thinking the very same thing." Jake answered. "I'm sure there must be something there we missed. Overton didn't give us a lot of time there."

"Why do you think Overton is so hot to arrest Morgan for this?" Fiona asked, walking over to join them at the counter.

Jake shrugged. "I have no idea. Either he is just really lazy and going with the newt theory, or there is something else that we don't know about."

"And what about the scarf?" Morgan asked, glancing at Fiona out of the corner of her eye. Fiona shook her head. She didn't trust Jake enough to tell him they had it yet.

"I don't know about that, either. She was strangled with something and it wasn't found at the crime scene. But did the killer take it, or did someone else get to the crime scene before the police? And why the anonymous tip about your garden? I have no idea." Jake spread his hands.

"So, when would be a good time to look over the crime scene?" Morgan asked.

Jake squinted one eye. "I have Saturday morning off. Maybe we could meet there early? I want to minimize the chance of people seeing us. It won't help our cause to have Overton know we went and looked at the scene together."

"Okay. We can open the shop a little late that day." Morgan looked at Fiona who nodded. "But exactly where is it?"

Jake pointed out the window toward the woods. "About a quarter mile that way. In between East Frazier Pasture and Sterns Road. Just meet me at the end of East Frazier's and we can walk up." He looked at his watch. "Say around six am?"

"Sounds good to me." Morgan said, looking at Fiona.

"Fine by me."

"Okay, see you girls later then." Jake smiled at Morgan and nodded at Fiona then headed out the door.

Fiona stared after him. She couldn't help but wonder what his motivation was for helping them. She still had concerns about trusting him, but she had to admit that it would be nice to have someone on the police force on "their side". That is, if he actually really was on their side.

Chapter Fifteen

Fiona stood on the porch looking toward Perkins Cove. Craning her neck, she leaned against the railing to get a better view. Her home was located on the point of land that shielded the cove from the Atlantic Ocean and, if she squinted, she could make out which boats were docked in the cove less than one quarter mile away.

"I think I see Josiah Littlefield on his boat." Fiona turned to Morgan who shooed Belladonna back inside as she stepped onto the porch.

"Well, now would be a perfect time to talk to him ... shall we?" Morgan spread her arm out indicating the steps that led down to the gravel driveway.

Fiona skipped down the steps and the sisters walked the length of the driveway side by side. As they stepped onto the pavement, Fiona breathed in the smell of fried clams.

"They're making clam rolls this early?" She looked at her watch, it was barely 8:00 a.m. Walking by the row of quaint shops, she peaked in the Clam Shack and saw they were already hard at work.

"I guess tourists like their clams for breakfast." Morgan shrugged as they continued past the tiny shops. The cove consisted of a modest harbor for boats and a small loop of about fifteen shops. Most of the shops were housed in tiny buildings that were once fisherman's shacks. It was a quaint old-Maine shopping and dining destination that tourists flocked to in the summer which made it rather crowded and impossible to find a parking spot.

Walking past the bait wharf, Fiona took a deep breath and reveled in the smell of dead fish and diesel. Most people found the two smells offensive, but to Fiona, it evoked childhood memories of fishing trips and lazy days.

She followed Morgan down the ramp to the dock. The tide was low. The smell of seaweed and clams hung in the air. Josiah Littlefield was busy cleaning off the deck of his lobster boat which was tied up to the dock.

"Hey, Josiah. We saw you down here and wanted to come and give our condolences about your sister-in-law." Fiona put her hand up to shade her eyes from the early morning sun as she looked up at Josiah on his boat.

"Ayuh." He kept cleaning the deck, not even looking up at them.

"I hope Ed is doing okay?" Fiona ventured.

Josiah turned and lifted a wooden lobster trap onto a stack of traps he had in the back of the boat. Fiona noticed the bulging muscles in his arms. He was strong for someone well into his seventies. *Strong enough to strangle Prudence?*

He came over to the side of the boat next to the girls. Leaning against the railing, he lifted his cap up to wipe the sweat from his forehead.

"I was out lobsterin' when it happened. Felt bad, I couldn't be with Ed right away. He's a might broken up about it. He dun like a talkin' much about it though. Seems to me he be much bettah off without her. No

117

mattah who killed her." He raised his eyebrows at Morgan.

"Oh, really? Why would he be better off?" Morgan asked.

Josiah shrugged. "She was a hard woman. Never lettin' Ed do nuttin' fun. She kept a tight fist on the money in that house."

Fiona nodded. "That can be hard on a man."

"Ayuh. But she musta been lettin' up some. He tol'e me just the other day 'bout how he was a gonna get hisself a boat."

"So, Prudence was loosening her grip on the money? Maybe she felt it was about time Ed had some fun in life." Fiona said.

Josiah squinted up into the sun. "Don't know. All's he said was he had some sorta plan."

He turned from the side of the boat, went over to the cabin and started the boat up.

"Just one more thing, Josiah," Fiona shouted over the roar of the engine.

Josiah turned and cocked an eyebrow at her.

"Was anyone with you when you were fishing that day?"

Josiah narrowed his eyes. Straightening his shoulders he said, "I dun know what you're gettin' at Ms. Blackmoore, but my deck hand Gordy Tuttle was with me same as he is every day. Now if you'll excuse me ..."

He untied the boat from the dock and motored off. Morgan turned to Fiona.

"We'll have to double check with Gordy, but if he was out fishing, he couldn't have killed Prudence."

"True, but one thing he said really worries me. He said that Ed had a "plan". I wonder if that plan included killing his wife.

Chapter Sixteen

"I'll drop you at the shop and then go talk to Ed by myself." Fiona glanced toward the passenger seat in time to see Morgan's jaw tighten.

"I think I should talk to him too."

"I don't think that's such a good idea. I mean, what if he's buying into this crap about you being the killer? It might not be good for you to show up on his doorstep."

Morgan sighed. "I guess you're right." She slumped back into the seat, biting her thumb nail.

"Don't worry, I'll get whatever I can out of him," Fiona said pulling up in front of *Sticks and Stones*.

Morgan slid out of the passenger seat, then shut the door and turned to look back in the window. "Good luck. And be careful— Ed might be a killer."

"Thanks. I will." Fiona put the truck in gear and headed east, toward Ed Littlefield's house. She shuddered as she passed the wooded area where Prudence was strangled.

Practically a stone's throw from their shop, the heavily wooded patch lay in between *Sticks and Stones* and the Littlefield's house which was on the street parallel to theirs.

Turning down the road, she saw a black SUV heading her way. Eli Stark. He glared at her through his open window when their cars passed each other.

Fiona felt her stomach tighten as she watched the back of his car in her rear view mirror. *What was he doing here?* Had he been to see Ed? And if so, why?

She pulled up in front of a small cottage whose wooden shakes were weathered to a dull gray by the harsh environment of sun and salt air.

Fiona got out of the truck, her heart beat picking up a few notches. Taking the homemade banana bread Celeste had given her, she made her way across the pine needle covered yard to the front door. Raising her fist, she knocked on the weathered wood.

Inside, the creaking of floorboards announced someone coming to the door. She shuffled her feet while she waited for it to open.

"Well, who is it now?" A harsh voice bellowed from inside the house.

"It's Fiona Blackmoore."

The door opened and Ed spoke to her from the other side of the screen door. "What do you want? Haven't your people done enough?"

Fiona straightened her back. "I just wanted to give my condolences and my sister, Celeste, baked this banana bread for you."

She held up the bread and Ed opened the door and grabbed it from her.

Eyeing it suspiciously he said. "One sister is a killer and the other sends bread to the victim's family?"

"Come on, Ed. You've known Morgan since she was a little girl. You were in the shop just days ago buying something from her. Sure, her and Prudence had their differences, but you know she's not a killer."

"I don't know anything anymore. Overton seems sure she did it." Fiona noticed his eyes were red. *Had he been crying?* Maybe he really was broken up about Prudence's death.

"Morgan's just as sorry about it as anyone."

Ed snorted. "Bullshit! I don't trust any of you Blackmoore girls, you need to get offa mah property!"

Fiona felt her cheeks grow warm. "Now wait just a minute Ed. There's no proof Morgan killed her. It could have been anyone ... even you."

"You better git girl, afore I make 'ya."

Fiona was too mad to heed his warning. "Where *were* you when Prudence was killed?" she blurted out.

Instead of answering, Ed reached over and grabbed something on the other side of the door. Fiona heard a click. Her heart froze when she realized she was staring down the business end of a shotgun.

She held up both hands, palms out. "Whoa there Ed ..."

Ed opened the screen door, advancing toward her. "I said git!"

Fiona backed down the steps, her hands still out in front of her, heart racing like a thoroughbred in the Kentucky Derby.

"Hey, I didn't mean to upset you." Fiona cautiously backed toward the direction of her truck. She remembered how Berta had said Ed was "gentle as a lamb". *Gentle my ass.* With a temper like that, she could picture him easily strangling Prudence in a fit of rage.

Fiona whipped around, ready to break into a run but her escape was blocked when she smacked into a brick wall that she swore hadn't been there before. At least it felt like a brick wall, but it wasn't. It was a solid, un-moveable mass of muscle—Jake Cooper.

Fiona's heart jerked in her chest. Jake put his hands on her waist to steady her and her stomach flip-flopped. Their eyes met just as she put her hand on his chest to push him away and she felt like time stood still.

"What are you doing here?" he asked. Fiona saw something flicker in his gray eyes. Amusement? Annoyance? Or was it something else?

"I ... I was just giving my condolences to Ed." Fiona sputtered. *Why did she feel like a child who got caught doing something wrong?*

Jake bent down, lowering his voice so that Ed couldn't hear him.

"Listen, Red. I know you're trying to get information from Ed, but I think it's best if you leave the interrogation to the experts."

Fiona's body tensed. There was nothing she hated more than someone trying to tell her what to do. She squirmed out of Jake's grip and took a step back.

"I don't need you telling me what to do. I have every right to extend my condolences to my neighbor." She stomped off toward her truck, ignoring Ed who was yelling at her not to come back. When she got to the truck, she turned to see Jake staring after her.

"And don't call me Red." She yelled over her shoulder as she jumped into the driver's seat, cranked the engine and sped off.

***

Jake stared after Fiona with an amused smile. She certainly was feisty. He liked that. His arms still tingled from when he had held her and looked down into her blue eyes. He wondered how those eyes could look both tough and vulnerable at the same time.

"What do *you* want?"

A voice shook him out of his thoughts and he turned to see Ed pointing the shotgun in his direction.

Jake felt a jolt of adrenalin rush through his veins. He held up his hands.

"Now Ed, put that thing down. I'm here on police business."

Ed narrowed his eyes at him, then, noticing Jake was in uniform, lowered the gun to his side.

"I brought Prudence's effects for you," Jake said solemnly.

"Oh." Ed lowered his head and Jake got a small box out of his car.

"Can we go inside?"

Ed nodded, leading the way up the steps and into the house.

The living room was simple, but clean. A plaid sofa sat against one wall, a lazy boy on the other. A small T.V. flickered images at the far end of the room. The coffee table held a cardboard pizza box and a bag of chips.

Ed motioned for Jake to sit on the couch and he did, gently placing the box on an empty spot on the coffee table in front of him.

Jake's stomach tightened as he took out his notebook. He always hated this part. You never knew how people were going to react.

Jake thought about all the people he'd questioned as a detective in Boston. When he took this job, he figured those days were over, but the small town didn't have a proper detective so the job fell to him, even if he didn't have the title.

"I have a few questions to ask you, if you don't mind."

Ed sat in the chair on the other side of the room, leaning forward with his elbows on his knees and surprised Jake with a question of his own.

"That Morgan Blackmoore, did she really kill my Prudy?" Ed wrinkled his brow at Jake.

Jake shrugged. "We don't know. Do *you* think she did it? What would her motive be?"

Ed looked down at the floor. "Well, I don' rightly know. I've known those Blackmoore girls since they were knee high. Morgan's always been sweet as pie. That redhead though, Fiona ... she's a might bit meddlesome." He glanced back at the front door and Jake couldn't help but smile at his description of Fiona.

"I'm afraid I might'a lost my tempah a bit with her, but she was askin' some personal questions." Ed turned back to Jake. "Prudy had her differences with the Blackmoore family, but that's been goin' on since their grandma was around."

"There's no hard evidence that connects Morgan to the murder," Jake said.

"But that newt? Everyone said they argued in the cafe and Morgan said she'da turn Prudy into a newt." Ed rubbed his stubble covered chin and narrowed his eyes at Jake. "D'ya think that Morgan really is a witch?"

Jake laughed. "Of course not." *That was ridiculous, wasn't it?*

Ed chuckled and looked down at his feet. "Yeah, I guess that's silly. But if not Morgan, then who?"

"That's what we are trying to find out. Do you know of anyone that might have wanted Prudence dead?"

Ed looked up at Jake and scrunched his wrinkled face while he thought for a minute. "No. Not really. I mean, she wasn't the easiest woman to get along with but I don't think that's a reason to kill someone. If t'were, someone woulda killed her a long time ago. "

"How were the two of you getting along?"

Ed's eyes went wide. "Hey, what are you tryin' ta say?"

Jake held up his hands. "These are standard questions, Ed," he said in a soothing voice. "I don't mean anything by them ... I have to ask."

"Oh, okay then. We got along fine. Fightin' like most couples at times."

"What did you fight about?"

Ed swatted the air with his hand. "We argued about selling this place. Eli Stark wants to knock it down and build condo's. I say take the money and enjoy it in our golden years, but Prudence wouldn't hear of it. It was an on-going battle but nothing I'd kill her over, if that's what cha' thinkin'." Ed looked up pointedly at Jake. "Besides, I was over at Cutty Marina when it happened. You can double check with them if you want."

Jake scratched a note in his notebook. "Ed, do you know why Prudence was in the woods that morning?"

"That twan't unusual. She did it every morning like clockwork; went for a walk down Shore Road, got a coffee at the cafe, then cut through the woods to get back home."

"So anyone would have known she would be there at that time of the morning?"

Ed looked at Jake, nodding slowly. "Yep, I guess so. But why would someone want to kill her?"

"That's what I intend to find out."

Jake motioned to the box on the table. "I need you to sign for this. You should probably make sure everything is there."

Ed stared at the box for a few seconds before slowly reaching over to pick it up. Jake could see his eyes filling with tears as he opened the lid. Ed did seem truly upset about his wife's death, but he'd seen many killers that were good actors. He couldn't cross him off the suspect list yet.

Lifting the lid of the small cardboard box, Ed reached in and took the items out one by one, laying them on the floor beside his chair.

Shirt, pants, shoes, wrist watch, socks. Ed pushed the rest of the items around in the box then jerked his head up to look at Jake.

"What's going on here?"

Jake wrinkled his brow. "Huh? What do you mean?"

"Everything's not here."

Jake got up crossing over to look in the box. "What's missing?"

"Pru's scarf. She always wore it. It had orange sunflowers on it."

Jake remembered the anonymous tip about the scarf buried in Morgan's garden.

"And her necklace."

"Necklace? What did it look like?"

"It was the letter 'P', for Prudence. In script. Darn thing was 18K gold. I gave it to her for her birthday. Cost me a pretty penny."

"Are you sure she had it on that day?"

Ed nodded. "She wore it every day, wouldn't leave the house without it." Ed narrowed his eyes at Jake, his face turning cloudy. "Do you think someone at the station stole it?"

Jake took a step back. "I'll surely check," he said in his best soothing voice which seemed to calm Ed down a bit. "But if they aren't at the station, and you don't have them here, there's only one possible explanation."

"What's that?"

"The killer has them."

Chapter Seventeen

Fiona ripped open the door to *Sticks and Stones*. Inside Morgan looked over at her expectantly, her brow creasing when she noticed Fiona's distress.

"What's the matter?"

"Oh, nothing ... well it's that damned Jake Cooper," she said storming into the shop and handing Morgan a tea from the cafe.

"What about him?"

"He showed up at Ed's and told me to stay out of police business!" Fiona's voice rose along with her anger as she paced the small shop.

"Come on, Fi, I'm sure he didn't mean it the way you are taking it." Morgan said soothingly while she searched her herb rack.

Fiona let out a sigh. Brushing the hair from her forehead she whirled to face Morgan.

"He did! And he called me Red. You know how I hate that."

Her sister's laughter only made Fiona angrier. She stood in the middle of the room, her feet planted firmly apart, glaring at Morgan.

"Sorry," Morgan said covering her mouth with her hand, "but you're acting like a child. Are you sure there isn't something else going on?"

Fiona thought about her sister's words as she took a sip of her latte. She did seem to get unusually angry at Jake. But that was because the man was annoying. What else could it be? Her brow furrowed as she remembered the warm tingle in her lower stomach when she had turned around to find herself practically in his arms.

"Here drink some of this." Morgan took the latte from Fiona's hand replacing it with a cup of herbal tea.

Fiona opened her mouth to protest, but Morgan raised her hand.

"Shush. This will help calm you. You can have the latte back later. Now tell me what you found out from Ed."

Fiona felt her stomach drop. She leaned against the counter while Morgan went back behind it and took a seat.

"I'm sorry, Morgan. I didn't really get any good information from him. He chased me out of there. Almost shot me, for crying out loud!"

"He did, why?" Morgan's ice blue eyes were as big as plates.

"Well, it might have been because I asked him where he was when Prudence was strangled." Fiona said sheepishly.

Morgan nodded. "Let me guess ... you did that with your usual lack of tact?"

Fiona grimaced. "Yeah. That's when he chased me out with his shotgun. I literally ran into Jake on the way out."

Morgan blew out a breath and pulled her long ebony hair back off her neck. "Well, if Jake was there after you, maybe he got something useful from Ed."

"Maybe. I still don't know if I trust him. Why do you think he'll be so helpful to us? Don't tell me you have the hots for him?" Fiona stared at Morgan wondering why her stomach was twisted in knots waiting for her answer. Must be this tea, she thought, looking down into the cup.

"No. I almost wish I was. But since Luke ... well ... I just haven't felt ..." Morgan turned and looked out the window. Fiona's heart ripped apart at the sadness on her sister's face.

Luke Hunter had been Morgan's high school sweetheart. They'd been a perfect couple from high school through their mid-twenties. Everyone assume they would get married, but then Luke felt the need to join the military to fight in the Middle East and he'd left Morgan back here with a broken heart.

Fiona wished her sister could move on, but part of her was glad that it wasn't going to be with Jake Cooper. Which she convinced herself was because she didn't quite trust him yet.

Morgan's eyes narrowed in on something she saw out the window. "Hey, is that Belladonna?"

Fiona came over to the window, looking in the direction of Morgan's gaze. She saw a white blur streak by. "I don't know. Is it? What would she be doing here?"

"I have no idea. She does seem to keep turning up here, though. I'll have to talk to Jolene about it. I'm worried Belladonna could get hurt coming all the way from our house with the traffic and all."

Fiona's stomach clenched picturing Belladonna dodging traffic on the busy main road. Their house was about a mile away. *Was that a long way for a cat to go?*

"Unless she comes down the Marginal Way," Fiona said. The Marginal Way was a footpath that went along the ocean's edge. The scenic route followed the cliffs from Perkins Cove where their house was to the center of Noquitt and was very popular with tourists. Belladonna could easily follow it to *Sticks and Stones* which was about midway on the path without ever seeing a car.

"Maybe. I hope so." Morgan opened the window wider, and stuck her head out. "Belladonna! Bella!"

"Meoooow."

"Oh, I guess that is her," Fiona said opening the door. The cat shot inside, then looked at the sisters innocently.

"Mew." She used a quiet, kitten like voice that would melt even the coldest heart. Fiona figured it was on purpose so as to avoid getting yelled at. She narrowed her eyes at the cat who proceeded to purr up at her and rub her head against her ankles.

The girls looked at each other shaking their heads.

"Well, at least she's safe in here now." Fiona watched Belladonna curl up in a sunny spot, marveling at how the cat could drop off to sleep in a second.

"Can I have my latte now?" She held out the teacup for a trade.

Morgan laughed and handed over the latte which Fiona took over to the microwave.

"Don't forget tomorrow we are going to check out the scene of the crime. So it would be great if you and Jake weren't at each other's throats." Morgan's blue eyes studied Fiona over the rim of her tea cup.

Fiona felt her heart clench. Morgan was right. She had to trust Jake to help them. It might be Morgan's only chance. "I know, I just don't understand why you trust him so much."

"Why *don't* you trust him?"

"I don't know. Why would he help us? We're strangers to him."

"Maybe he just wants to do the right thing. He said he doesn't trust Overton and doesn't think the investigation is being run properly."

"Or maybe Overton has him helping us as a plant. To find out what we know or get some evidence to incriminate you."

Morgan bit her lower lip. "I don't think so, I have a gut feeling about Jake Cooper and my gut feelings are usually right."

Morgan stared at Fiona so long that Fiona started to squirm. "What?"

"I was wondering if maybe your resistance to Jake is something else. How long has it been since you broke up with Kevin?"

Fiona felt her heart jerk at the mention of her ex-fiance. She'd been engaged to Kevin O'Laughlin for four years ... until she found him cheating on her two years ago. It had been heart breaking and she'd vowed never to let anyone hurt her like that again.

"What's that got to do with anything?" She crossed her arms across her chest.

"Maybe nothing. But I've seen the way Jake looks at you and I was wondering if maybe the resistance you feel is actually an attraction."

"What?" Fiona felt her face grow warm. *Could Morgan be right?* Her sister had an uncanny way of digging to the root of people's feelings.

Morgan just shrugged and starting grinding some herbs with her pestle.

Fiona felt flustered. She went over to her workbench and fiddled with her jewelers tools. "It's not."

"Huh?" Morgan looked up at her.

"An attraction. I mean, I barely know the guy," Fiona answered.

"Of course," Morgan said. "Just as long as you guys get along I don't really care what it is. I saw Overton at the cafe and he made some remark about how I should still be in jail. I really hope Jake can help us find something to put us on the track of the real killer and get Overton off my back."

Fiona stared down at the necklace she was working on without really seeing it. Her mind was too busy thinking about Overton and why he was so hot to frame Morgan. Maybe if they could figure that out, it would lead them in the direction of the real killer.

She raked her fingers through her red curls and made a vow to give Jake Cooper a chance—for Morgan's sake and nothing else.

What Morgan had said earlier about her resistance really being attraction was ridiculous. And even if it was true, she had no intention of following through with it ... no matter how deep his gray eyes were or how good he smelled.

Chapter Eighteen

The next morning started out unusually hot for mid spring. Fiona dressed in khaki Capri's, a black tank top and black and white polka-dot Keds for their trip to the woods. Pulling her red curls into a pony tail that sat high on her head and hung halfway down her back, she trotted down to the kitchen to meet Morgan.

Her older sister was already in the kitchen, holding a tea bag in her hand as she watched the microwave heat a cup of water. Her jet black hair hung from a similar pony tail. She had on a similar pair of Keds in navy blue to top off her outfit of denim capris and white tank top.

Fiona looked down at her outfit, then at Morgan. "I guess this is standard crime scene visiting garb."

Morgan laughed. "I guess so. It seems like it's going to be hot today so I didn't want to get overheated."

Fiona nodded. "Are you ready?"

"Yep. Let's take my car." Morgan grabbed her cup.

"Okay, but I need to stop at the cafe and get a latte."

Five minutes later, Morgan pulled her Toyota up to the pre-arraigned meeting spot at the end of East Frazier Pasture Road. Jake was already there leaning casually against a beat up gold and black Suburban. Fiona tried not to notice that his tee-shirt was just a bit tight against his muscular chest. She gulped down her latte and got out of the car.

"You guys ready?" He pushed himself off the car starting toward them.

"Ready as we'll ever be." Morgan said.

The three fell in line walking the short distance to an opening in the woods.

"It's through here." Jake gestured to a barely visible path.

As they walked further into the woods, the trees became more dense and Fiona felt the temperature drop a few degrees. They had walked about a quarter mile when they came to an area still marked with yellow crime scene tape. Inside the tape, a large area of leaves and pine needles were disturbed where an obvious struggle had gone on.

Fiona looked around to get her bearings. They were in the deepest part of the woods with no houses visible.

"So Prudence's house is in that direction." She pointed to the North.

Jake nodded. "And the cafe is in that direction," he said pointing West.

Morgan turned in a circle inside the taped off area. "Where did the killer come from?"

Jake shrugged.

"Well, *Sticks and Stones* must be over there," Morgan said pointing to the South. "But that morning I was coming from the cafe, so if I killed her, I would have had to walk up the same path Prudence did, strangle her, then run off that way."

"You wouldn't have had enough time to do that." Jake said, "I mean, if the time you say you got to *Sticks and Stones* is right."

Fiona glared at Jake. "Of course, it is. We know the exact time she got there. Plus my latte was warm."

Jake held up his hands. "I know, Red, just saying what a prosecuting lawyer might say."

Fiona pursed her lips together. *Did he just call her Red, again?* But instead of getting angry, she just smiled. He was right, of course. They had to consider what a prosecutor might use against them.

"I don't know how any of that will help us now." Morgan pushed some of the leaves aside with her foot. "We need to be looking for clues the police might have missed."

"Speaking of which, I took the box of Prudence's effects to Ed yesterday and a couple of things were missing. We don't have them down at the station, so we should be on the lookout for them here. If they aren't here, then the killer likely has them."

"What are they?" Fiona looked up at Jake who had his head down, scanning the ground.

"A gold necklace with the letter 'P', and a scarf with sunflowers on it."

Fiona's heart clenched. She looked over at Morgan. *Should they tell him about the scarf?* Morgan widened her eyes and nodded her head toward Jake. Fiona knew exactly what she meant. They *had* to tell him.

Fiona cleared her throat and Jake narrowed his eyes at her.

"What?"

"We know where one of those is."

He raised his eyebrows looking from Morgan to Fiona.

"The scarf ... it really was buried in the garden."

"So the tip was real?"

"I guess so. It just so happened I found it earlier that day, so when you guys came to dig up the garden I had already removed it."

Jake sighed. "So you tampered with evidence."

Fiona bit her bottom lip. "Well, technically. But I didn't know it was evidence when I dug it up ... sort of."

"Sort of?" Jake looked at her incredulously.

"What she means is that she knew it was Prudence's scarf, but didn't realize that was what she had been strangled with."

Jake ran his hands through his short cropped hair. "Do you know how it got there?"

"No idea."

"I'm going to need to see it. There could be evidence on there."

"Okay." Fiona felt her stomach sinking. She hoped she hadn't done anything to harm Morgan's case.

"The only problem is that now we can't really turn it in to the police."

"Maybe we shouldn't have told you," Fiona said. "We don't want you to get into trouble."

"Now that you do know about it ... if you don't tell the police that could look bad for you," Morgan added, her blue eyes full of concern.

Jake just shrugged. "Well, what I'm doing now doesn't look so good, so I guess it really doesn't matter. Besides, I'm on the side of finding out the truth ... I'm not sure what side Overton is on."

"We don't have the other item." Morgan added in a small voice.

"Is there anything else you guys need to tell me?"

Both girls shook their heads.

"Well, just one tiny thing." Fiona winced at Jake's look of exasperation.

"What?"

"We talked to Ed's brother, Josiah, yesterday and he said Ed was planning on buying a boat," Fiona said. "I wonder if he had a big insurance policy on Prudence?"

"Ed didn't mention that to me yesterday, but it didn't really come up in the conversation either. He claims he was at Cutty Marina when she was killed, so he has an alibi I can check."

"Josiah claims to have an alibi too. Says he was out lobstering and his deck hand can verify it."

"Okay, I'll check into that," Jake said. "Let's just get on with searching this area."

They put their heads down and started looking. Fiona pushed the leaves around with her feet disturbing a few little orange fire newts that were hanging around underneath.

"There's lots of newts here. Do you guys think one could have just crawled into Prudence's mouth on its own?"

"That would be quite a coincidence, wouldn't it?" Jake asked.

"Yes," Morgan answered. Then she laughed. "That would also be really bad luck, because if it wasn't for the newt, I don't think I would have been implicated."

Fiona wrinkled her brow. "That would really be a bummer, if it was just a coincidence."

They passed the next half hour in silence, each of them busy with their heads bent toward the ground, sweeping the area with their feet. Fiona concentrated on trying to avoid stepping on newts while she focused on looking for anything out of the ordinary.

"Meow." Fiona whirled toward the direction of the sound. She felt her stomach lurch when she saw Belladonna standing about ten feet away, out of the crime scene taped area. *This was getting kind of creepy. The cat was showing up everywhere.*

"Belladonna!" Morgan rushed over to the cat who looked up at her adoringly, then head butted her shin while Morgan bent down to pet her.

"Is that your cat?" Jake asked.

"Yep. She seems to like to wander around outside, even though we try to keep her in the house." Fiona joined Jake in walking over to where Morgan and Belladonna where.

The three of them stood laughing at the cat as she played in the leaves. First she batted some leaves with her paw, and as they were swirling around, she pounced on them, sliding this way and that.

She leaped in the air, pouncing on a pile of leaves, then batted something at the bottom which slid out of the pile. Fiona saw a reflection of sunlight glint off the object.

"Hey wait a minute." She bent down and grabbed it before Belladonna could bat at it again. Straightening up, she stared at the nickel sized object. Shaped like a crescent moon with a tiny black jewel on each end, it was some sort of silver colored metal.

"What's that?" Morgan wrinkled her brow holding out her hand.

Fiona handed it over. "I don't know."

Jake looked down at the ring. "I'm not sure but I think it might be some sort of jewelry people wear in a piercing."

"Ewww." Morgan dropped it, wiping her hands on her pants.

"Wait. That could be evidence." Jake bent down to pick it up. "It's too small for fingerprints, but maybe if we can find out who owns it, they might know something about the murder."

Fiona took another look at it. "If it's for a piercing, I bet Celeste knows more about it. I'll ask her."

She held out her hand palm up and Jake dropped the ring into it. She gave it one final look, and slid it into her front pocket.

"Oh crap, I'm late!" Morgan stared at the watch on her slim wrist.

"Late?" Fiona screwed up her face, looking at her sister.

"Yes, I have an important appointment." She turned to Jake. "Jake, can you drop Fiona at the shop when you guys are done?"

Jake cocked an eyebrow at Morgan, then turned to Fiona. "Sure."

"What? Wait a minute—"

But Fiona's protests were cut off by Morgan who raised her hand. "Sorry, gotta run." Fiona watched open-mouthed as her sister swooped up the cat and took off down the path.

Swiveling around to face Jake, Fiona realized he had the same "deer in the headlights" look on his face that she had on hers. The woods seemed oddly quiet. No birds chirping. No squirrels scurrying in the leaves.

Fiona suddenly became very aware that she was alone with Jake. She felt awkward and excited, like a schoolgirl on her first date. She shook her head to clear the thoughts. She was no schoolgirl, and this was no date.

Finally, Jake cleared his throat. "We should search more over here. I don't know if that jewelry has anything to do with the murder but, if it does, there could be something more."

Fiona nodded and resumed the task of scuffling through the leaves. After a while, the sun started to warm the woods to an unbearable heat. Her skin was slick with sweat and black flies buzzed around her head.

"I haven't found anything else." Jake straightened up, his slightly damp shirt clinging to him. Fiona tried not to stare as she swatted a swarm of black flies away from her face.

"Me either."

Jake slapped the side of his neck where a black fly had bitten him. "These flies are getting nasty. How about we call it quits and get an ice cream?"

Fiona looked at him uncertainly. "Ice cream?"

"Yeah, you know that cold, sweet stuff. Come on, it will taste good ... and I promise not to call you Red."

Fiona laughed. "Okay, that sounds good, but I need to get to the shop by eleven."

"No problem."

Fiona's stomach felt like butterflies had hatched inside it as she led the way down the path. She didn't know if it was because she still didn't trust Jake, or if the butterflies were caused by something else. He had certainly been working hard to help them find something this morning and he was risking his job to do it. Surely that meant that he was on their side?

Chapter Nineteen

Fiona savored the cold, creamy sweetness of the maple walnut ice cream on her tongue. She looked across the redwood picnic table at Jake who worked on his own cone — a double scoop of mint chocolate chip.

Watching his tongue deftly carve a trough in the side of the extra-large scoop, she felt her mouth water--and not for the ice cream, either. She jerked her eyes away and tried to distract herself with conversation.

"So, what did you do in Boston?"

Jake blotted the ice cream off his lips with a small napkin before he replied. "I was a detective."

"Oh, things must seem awfully dull up here to you, then."

Jake shrugged. "It's not that bad. Things in Boston can be a lot more dangerous ... as my partner found out."

"Oh?" Fiona cocked an eyebrow at him.

Jake shifted his gaze. A dark cloud crept into his eyes as he looked out over the parking lot. "He was killed while we were working on a case."

Fiona's stomach dropped at the look of sadness on his face. She noticed a tic in his cheek before his face softened and he turned back to her.

"Do you like it here?" she asked, scraping a mound of ice cream into her mouth with her teeth.

"Sure, I like the small town atmosphere. The guys at the station are all nice. Except Overton. It's more laid back here. Boston was hectic."

He held his cone up and licked a few drips of ice cream that were racing toward his hand. "What about you? You've lived here all your life, right?"

Fiona smiled. "Yep. And my parents, and their parents, and their parents. My ancestors were the first ones to build a house in this town."

"You never wanted to live anywhere else?"

Fiona crunched into her cone. "No. I've never even thought about it. I love being on the ocean and, of course, my sisters are all here. The only time I've ever lived away was for a few months in New York when I got my gemologist license. I learned I'm not much of a city girl."

Jake nodded, shoving the rest of his cone in his mouth then wiping the drips from his hands with a napkin.

Fiona daintily munched her cone down. "You don't think Overton will be able to pin Prudence's murder on Morgan, do you?"

Jake shrugged. "I don't think so, but what I would really like to know is why he would even want to. Did Morgan piss him off somehow?"

"Not that I know of. He only came to town about four years ago, but he's had it in for us ever since. My youngest sister, Jolene, got into a bit of trouble with the law in high school, but nothing out of the ordinary. Nothing to make him hate us."

"I guess we'll just have to outsmart him."

"That shouldn't be too hard." Fiona pushed the tip of the cone into her mouth and chewed.

"We do have another lead to follow up on, too: The necklace with the 'P'." Jake pressed his lips together and looked out toward the road. "We just need to figure out a way to find out who has it."

"Or had it," Fiona said snapping her fingers.

"What?"

"What would the killer want with it? Would they keep it?"

"Well some of them keep things as a souvenir, but that's usually serial killers and I don't think we are dealing with that here."

"So they probably took it for the monetary value which means they would try to sell it, and it just so happens that one of my oldest friends owns a pawn shop in town.

Jake raised his eyebrows. "We should check that out."

"We can talk to him tonight, if you want." Fiona's heart skipped in anticipation of his answer.

"Sounds good." Jake looked at his watch. "We better go." Then he narrowed his eyes at her and pointed to his mouth.

"Huh?" Fiona's brows knit together. Her heart stopped when Jake reached over the table to wipe a smudge of ice cream from the corner of her mouth.

Her eyes widened in shock when he licked the ice cream off his thumb. "The maple walnut is good here. I'll have to get that next time." Then he stood and led the way to his Suburban.

Jake's Suburban sat high off the ground, but Fiona's long legs allowed her to swing herself easily into the passenger side. She rolled down the window, preferring the feel, and smell, of the ocean breeze to air conditioning. The truck gave a smooth ride despite its dilapidated appearance and she liked the way the Suburban sat high on the road, even if it was a bit beat up inside. She was surprised to discover she felt a little sad when Jake pulled up in front of *Sticks and Stones*.

"Thanks for the ice cream." She unbuckled her seat belt and grappled with the door handle. She pulled and tugged, shoved her shoulder against the door but it wouldn't open.

"Sorry, that door sticks sometimes. Let me help." Her heart rate kicked into overdrive as Jake leaned across her to push the handle. He was close, his chest almost touching hers. The smell of warm spice, salt and mint teased her nostrils.

He looked down at the handle, fiddled with it, then turned to look at her, his face mere inches from hers. She saw a spark of lust in his eyes and held her breath. His eyes locked on hers for a few seconds, then dropped to her lips. *Was he going to kiss her?* She was surprised to realize every nerve in her body wanted him to.

He took a deep breath and shoved the door open, pulling back to his side of the truck.

Fiona slid out, letting out her own breath in a whoosh. She shut the door, and turned to look back through the window. "See you tonight, then?"

"Yep. I also want to take a look at that scarf." Jake ran a hand through his hair.

"Okay. You wanna come buy my house around six? I'll talk to Cal and make sure he'll be open."

"Great. See you then." Jake turned the key in the ignition and Fiona walked up the path to the shop cursing her hormones ... and her heart ... for the way they were acting.

Her mind drifted back to what Morgan had said about how it had been a long time since the whole mess with Kevin. Maybe it *was* time to move on. Fiona looked back to see Jake staring after her, she gave a final wave then turned back up the path to the shop.

Chapter Twenty

Fiona fidgeted at the front door, checking her watch and peering down the long gravel road.

"You don't have to stand watch. He'll get here when he gets here." The voice made her jump. Morgan had snuck up behind her in the large foyer.

"I was just nervous about showing him the scarf." Fiona cursed her pale coloring as she felt her cheeks grow warm.

Morgan let out a trill of laughter. "Right. I'm sure that's it."

"Oh, here he is." Fiona opened the door and walked onto the porch watching Jake pull his truck to a stop and get out.

"Hi." Jake's long legs carried him up on the porch.

Morgan appeared in the doorway. "Hi, Jake."

"Hey, Morgan. Did you guys talk to your pawn shop friend?"

"I called him, but he's in Aruba with one of his many lady friends. Won't be back 'til the day after tomorrow, but he said he'd be happy to talk to us then," Fiona said then turned to Morgan. "I thought Cal might know if someone pawned Prudence's necklace."

Morgan nodded. "Good idea."

"Can I see the scarf?" Jake lowered his voice at the last word and glanced over his shoulder.

"Sure, come on in." Fiona opened the door, ushered Jake in and the three of them went up the wide front staircase and down the East hall to Fiona's room.

Fiona noticed that Jake looked out of place amidst the Victorian floral wallpaper and bedding. For a second she considered redecorating, then pushed the thought aside. She'd laid the scarf out on the bed and the three of them stood there staring at it.

"I don't see any blood or anything. Can fabric hold a fingerprint?"

"Unfortunately, no," Jake lifted the scarf gently, then let it flutter back to the bed. "Are you sure she was wearing this?"

Morgan nodded. "She had it on in the cafe."

"And I saw it on her when she was walking that morning." Fiona said. "It's pretty hard not to notice it."

Jake looked out the window at the Atlantic Ocean. "So it must have been the killer ... or the police that planted it. No one else would have had access to it, unless she went home, took it off, and then went out again."

"I don't think she'd have had time."

"No, me either."

"Well, apparently staring at the scarf isn't going to give us any clues." Jake turned to Fiona. "Did you ask your sister about that jewelry we found in the woods?"

"Not yet, she was meditating when we got home, but she's probably done now."

They started to leave the room, then Jake grabbed Fiona's elbow sending tingles up and down her arm. "You should hide the scarf. Just in case something crazy happens and they get a search warrant."

Fiona's stomach clenched. "A search warrant? Could they do that?"

Jake shrugged. "You never know. Better to be safe than sorry."

Fiona looked back at the scarf making a mental note to put it back under the floorboard after everyone was gone. She didn't want to give away her hiding spot, it had been her secret place since she was a kid and no one knew about it—not even Morgan.

They went down the side stairs, heading toward the back of the house. Fiona peeked into the library where Celeste preferred to meditate and found it empty except for the shelves filled with antique leather-bound books.

"She's probably in the kitchen," she said continuing forward.

In the kitchen they found Celeste dressed in yoga pants and a stretchy top, running what looked like grass through the juicer into a small glass.

"Oh, hi," Celeste smiled at them. "Want some?"

She held up the glass full of murky green goo and the three of them shook their heads.

"Celeste, you remember Jake Cooper? He's helping us figure out who framed me," Morgan said.

Celeste eyed Jake suspiciously, then nodded a greeting.

Fiona slipped the jewelry out of her pocket. "Celeste, do you know what this is?"

Celeste leaned over and took a quick look at the item. "Sure, its a nose ring."

"Nose ring?" Fiona stared at the ring as Celeste handed it back. "Really? It looks too big."

"It's not for the side, it goes in the middle —in your septum."

"Eww, in the middle of your nose? Like a bull? That seems like it would hurt." Fiona wrinkled her brow at the piece of jewelry.

"Who wears those? I don't see too many people with a nose ring like that around town."

"Mostly young kids."

"Yeah, a few of my friends from High School have them," Jolene said from the doorway. "Personally I think they are gross."

"What would it be doing in the woods?"

"The kids spend a lot of time in there, drinking and avoiding the police. It might not have anything to do with Prudence's murder, especially since we didn't find it near the scene. Maybe some kid just lost it while they were partying," Jake said.

"That could happen, but it's actually pretty hard to get those things out." Jolene came closer to take a look at the ring.

Fiona put it on the counter. "Okay, well this may or may not be a clue. So now where does that leave us?"

"We don't have much, an old scarf and a nose ring. I'm not sure how any of those point to our main suspects—Berta, Josiah and Ed." Morgan raised her eyebrows and looked at the others. "It doesn't look promising."

"Actually, it's even worse." Jake said. The girls swiveled their heads in his direction and he continued. "I checked with the hospital and Berta did sprain her wrist last week, so I don't think she would have physically been able to strangle Prudence. Plus she was at the hairdresser at the time of death. Josiah's deck hand verifies they were out fishing that day and two other lobstermen also saw his boat off the point at the time of the murder. Ed's alibi with Cutty Marine checks out too. So, looks like none of them could have done it."

Fiona felt her stomach drop. She stared at Jake incredulously.

"Well, if Berta didn't do it, Josiah didn't do it and Ed didn't do it, then who the hell did?"

Chapter Twenty One

Anastasia LePage fluttered into *Sticks and Stones* in a flurry of chiffon and gemstones.

"I do hope you girls can help me."

She stared over her magenta bifocals, aiming her gaze first at Morgan and then Fiona.

"Of course we can, Annie." Fiona smiled at their eccentric customer. The wealthy octogenarian had discovered *Sticks and Stones* on a vacation to Noquitt several years ago. Being a true believer in the healing power of herbs and crystals, she usually made many purchases a year. Fiona and Morgan were happy to give her exactly what she needed.

"What is it you need?" Morgan came around to the other side of the counter and pulled out a chair, motioning for Anastasia to sit.

"Well, as you girls know, I'm getting on in years. I'll be eighty-two in December." She winked at Fiona. "And I'm just dying to have a great-grandchild."

Fiona raised an eyebrow at her. "How can we help?"

"My granddaughter's been married for two years and I'm very disappointed that she hasn't produced a child." Anastasia leaned closer toward the girls and lowered her voice. "I'm afraid she might need some help."

At the perplexed look on the girls' faces, she continued, "Do you girls have herbs and crystals that help with fertility?" She waved her bejeweled fingers around the room, indicating the shelves of herbs and cases of crystals.

"Oh, yes, of course!" Fiona laughed.

"Then that's what I need for my granddaughter. Can we package them up like gifts? I don't want her feelings to be hurt."

"Of course." Morgan went over to her herb rack. "I can make a bottle of evening primrose oil she could use for skin care and I can make some custom tea bags with dong quai and false unicorn root. Those are great for fertility."

"I can create a necklace, earring and bracelet set with moonstones, rose quartz and amethyst. Those stones go perfectly together and they will help with fertility too."

Anastasia clapped her hands together. "Perfect! I knew I could count on you girls." Stabbing her cane onto the floor, she pulled herself up. "When can I pick them up?"

"I'll probably need a couple of days, what about you Fi?"

"I have a few other orders to work on, so about four days. Could you pick them up on Friday?"

"Certainly. I'm here for the entire summer, so no rush." Anastasia said graciously as she turned toward the door.

"I hope you dear girls haven't been hurt by all that dreadful business with the Littlefield woman." She half turned to face them.

"Not too much. We'll be fine."

"It was quite disturbing. My cottage is only a stone's throw from where it happened." Anastasia shuddered.

"Oh, that must have been scary for you." Fiona narrowed her eyes. "You didn't see or hear anything, did you?"

"As a matter of fact, I did."

Morgan's eyes widened. "You did? What?"

"I was having tea on my porch, as is my custom in the morning, when a young man burst out of the woods and ran off down the road toward the ocean. It quite startled me. I nearly had a heart attack."

"What time was that?"

Anastasia wrinkled her brow looking up at the ceiling. "Well, it must have been around quarter past eight or a bit earlier. I usually take my tea between eight and eight thirty."

Fiona felt her heart beat racing. That was just about when Prudence was killed! "Did you see what he looked like?"

"My eyes aren't too good these days, dear. All I saw was that he had one of those hooded sweatshirts, but as he ran by the hood fell back and I noticed he had one of those awful tattoos."

"A tattoo? Of what?"

"I'm not sure. It looked like a lightning bolt or something."

"Anastasia, did you tell the police about this man?"

"The police? No. They didn't even bother to talk to me," she said waving her hand in dismissal. Then she turned the knob and opened the door. "Well, you girls have a lovely day."

Fiona shot Morgan a raised eyebrow look. "A young man running out of the woods right at the time of Prudence's death? Maybe he saw something?"

"Or killed her."

Fiona felt a chill run up her spine. "Either way, one thing is for sure, we need to find out who has a lightening tattoo on their neck and pay them a visit."

Chapter Twenty Two

Fiona liberated the steamed clam from its shell and carefully peeled the membrane from its neck. She dunked it in broth, then butter and popped it in her mouth making nummy noises as the sweet, salty steamer slid down her throat.

"These are awesome, thanks for bringing them home from work," she said to Jolene, seated across from her at the wrought iron table.

"Yes, thanks," Morgan and Celeste echoed her words.

Jolene looked up from dunking her own clam and smiled. "You're welcome."

The four of them sat on the back patio in the fading evening sun. Situated high on a cliff, the patio sat at the point where the water from the Atlantic flowed into Perkins Cove, giving them a three sided view of ocean.

The sound of seagulls and sting of the salt air were a perfect backdrop for the sister's to indulge themselves in the ritual of eating steamed clams. She loved simple times like this with her sisters. Which reminded her, there might not be more of them if Morgan ended up in jail.

"We got another lead in Prudence's murder today," Fiona said.

Celeste raised her brows. "You did? What?"

"A customer is staying in one of the cottages near the woods where Prudence was killed and she saw someone run out from there. We might need help in identifying him." Fiona looked down at Belladonna, who had appeared at Morgan's side begging for a clam.

"Sure, anything. Do you think he's from town? What does he look like?"

"I don't know if he's from town, but the woman said he had a very distinctive tattoo on the side of his neck. I was hoping that, if we all ask around, we can figure out who he is."

Morgan threw Belladonna a clam. Fiona watched the cat pounce on it, sniff it, then flick her tail and walk away.

"She said it looked like a lightning bolt." Fiona looked up to see Jolene's eyes grow wide.

"I think I know who that is," Jolene said dropping her clam. "Joshua Gray." She looked around the table. "I told you guys about him before, remember. He's kind of a bad apple. He also wears one of those nose rings like you had last night."

The table went silent.

Fiona's heart stopped. "Do you know where he lives?"

"Over in Wells, right on the town line. He lives in a mobile home, but not in the trailer park, about a mile past it."

Fiona's chair scraped the concrete patio as she got up.

"Where are you going?" Morgan squinted up at her.

"To pay Mr. Gray a visit."

Fiona sprinted into the kitchen and grabbed her keys. Morgan ran in behind her.

"Wait, don't you think we should call Jake before we go?"

Fiona slowed down. They probably *should*, but that would waste time. Then again, if Joshua Gray was a killer, it might not be very smart to go there by themselves.

"You can call him in the car on the way over." Fiona yelled over her shoulder at Morgan as she sprinted for the front door.

***

The decades old single-wide trailer sat in the shadow of the woods, its door slightly ajar and angled on its hinges. Grimy curtains fluttered out the kitchen window as if trying to escape. Fiona's heartbeat raced as she approached it.

"Joshua?"

She was met with silence. Unusual silence. No chirping birds, no scurrying squirrels. The only sound was the door squeaking as the breeze moved it back and forth.

Fiona found the silence unnerving. Her heartbeat kicked up another notch as she stepped up to the trailer door and knocked on it.

"Joshua Gray, are you in there?"

Nothing.

Over to her left, Morgan had ventured to the end of the trailer and was rounding the corner.

Fiona's chest tightened as she put her foot on the step and poked her head into the trailer through the open door.

"Hello?"

The 60 inch flat screen television that took up one whole end of the living room space was at odds with the rest of the decor which could only be described as junk. The floor was strewn with beer bottles and trash. Dirty clothes were draped on a stained lazy-boy chair and the sink and counters were hidden by piles of dirty dishes.

"Josh, are you in here?" Fiona called out again, just in case he was in one of the other rooms.

"I don't think he's going to answer." Fiona's heart lurched, she wheeled around to see Morgan, white faced and shaking.

"Why? What happened?"

Morgan pointed to the side of the trailer and Fiona walked in the direction she indicated, her legs getting heavier with each step.

She rounded the corner.

Her heart lurched when she saw it. A body lay on the ground amidst a pile of leaves that were stained dark red.

Fiona gasped as she took it all in. Legs splayed at an impossible angle. Torso drenched in blood. Sightless eyes staring up at the sky. And a lightning bolt tattoo clearly visible on the neck.

Fiona gasped. Her hands flew to her mouth, then she turned and ran back to join Morgan. Josh Gray wouldn't be answering any questions for them, after all.

***

Fiona sat on the trailer steps with her head between her knees. She was barely aware of the blaring sirens and sound of cars pulling into the driveway. The clams that tasted so good going down earlier in the evening were threatening to make a comeback and she was certain they wouldn't be as tasty on the way up.

A cool hand on the back of her neck caused her to jerk her head up.

"Are you okay?" Jake looked down at her with concern in his eyes.

She nodded, too queasy to speak. He massaged her neck while Overton barked orders behind the trailer.

Finally, the nausea subsided and she lifted her head to see a flurry of police activity going on around her.

Jake squatted down so that his face was level with hers. "What are you doing here?"

"A customer at the shop said she saw a guy with a tattoo on his neck run out of the woods the morning Prudence was killed. It just so happened Jolene recognized the description of the tattoo and pointed us here."

"So you came here to confront him by yourselves? Do you know how dangerous that is?" A cloud of anger passed over Jake's face.

"We called you on the way," Fiona winced. Her impulsive actions often got her into trouble.

Jake scrubbed his hands through his hair. "It's just that you could have gotten hurt. This guy could be a killer." He touched her arm and her stomach did a somersault making her feel a little queasy again but for a different reason. "I'd never forgive myself if something happened to you."

Fiona's heart clenched. She opened her mouth to say something.

"Cooper, get over here." Overton bellowed from the side of the trailer.

Jake did a half shrug, and put his hand on her knee. "I guess we'll talk later." He stood up and walked toward Overton.

Fiona stared after him. *Talk later?* She was busy wondering just what that meant when Overton strolled by on his way to Morgan who was giving a statement to Brody Hunter.

"Well, well, look who seems to be mixed up in another murder." Overton stood in front of Morgan, a smug look plastered on his face.

Fiona stood up and crossed the yard, putting her arm around her sister. "What are you talking about? We came to visit and found a body. Morgan called 911 for crying out loud!"

Overton took the toothpick out of his mouth. "A perfect way to cover up that you're the killer."

"That's ridiculous!"

"Is it? I think it gives me enough to bring your sister in and question her."

"What?" Fiona sputtered. "Why would Morgan want to kill Josh?"

Overton narrowed his eyes. "I don't know. Maybe he saw her kill Prudence and she was trying to silence him. Which means you're probably in on it with her. Looks like I'll have to bring you both in." Overton crooked his fingers at another one of the uniforms who scurried over.

"Cuff these two and put them in the car."

Brody eyed Morgan uncertainly. The officer grabbed Fiona's elbow and she jerked it away.

"Unhand my clients!"

Delphine Jones came flying up the driveway, her purple and orange caftan billowing out like the mainsail of a frigate.

Brody and the other officer stopped in mid-cuff, looking between Delphine and Overton in confusion.

"You again." Overton shoved the toothpick back in his mouth.

"What's going on here?" Delphine demanded.

"We came to visit and found him dead, then called 911." Fiona nodded toward the side of the trailer where Josh's body lay.

Delphine turned to Overton. "My clients were simply reporting that they found the body, like any law abiding citizen. I hardly see how that gives you cause to handcuff them."

Overton swooshed the toothpick around in his mouth and glared at Delphine.

Fiona watched the two of them stare each other down. Delphine must have won because Overton eventually said, "Let them go. We can take their statements here."

Then he turned on his heel and stormed back behind the trailer.

***

Fiona and Morgan suffered through a battery of questions. By the time they were done Fiona wanted to take Overton's toothpick and shove it down his throat. Thankfully, Delphine stayed by their side to make sure the interrogation didn't veer off track.

In between the questions, the medical examiner had arrived and was updating Overton with information. Like the size of the knife, the fact it was serrated only three quarters of the way and that it had a distinctive scrolled hilt. Fiona filed it all away for later use, figuring it might come in handy to identify the killer.

Fiona caught herself looking for Jake several times. Overton had kept him busy investigating the scene but the few times their eyes met, Fiona had felt a familiar zing at the pit of her stomach. Her heart warmed knowing Jake was looking out for them.

"Looks like we're done ... for now." Overton snapped his notebook shut and glared at the girls.

"So my clients are free to go, then, right?" Delphine said it as more of a statement than a question.

Overton gave her a look of pure hatred and Fiona knew that if it wasn't for Delphine, she and Morgan might be spending the night in a cell. She wondered if Delphine had something on Overton that caused him to tread carefully around her and toe the line.

"They can go," he said to Delphine, then turned to Morgan and Fiona. "But don't leave town."

Fiona made a face behind his back. "Don't leave town? How cliche can you get?" Morgan and Delphine laughed.

"My job here is done, so I'll be on my way. If Overton harasses you about this any more, call me right away." Delphine turned and headed toward her car.

Fiona watched Delphine flutter down the driveway. The woman had really come in handy. Fiona congratulated herself for having the good sense to hire her even as her mind tried to calculate how much of the five thousand dollar retainer they'd already blown through.

"Let's go home, I'm exhausted." Morgan covered a yawn with her hand.

Fiona glanced around the yard. Only a few cops remained.

"Jake already left with Brody," Morgan said looking at Fiona out of the corner of her eye.

Fiona's cheeks burned. "I wasn't looking for Jake."

"Right." Morgan led the way to the car.

"It's kind of scary. I've lived here my whole life and I don't think there's been more than four or five murders the whole time. Now there have been two in less than a week. They have to be related." Morgan snapped the seatbelt into place.

"It would seem that way, but why would someone want to kill Josh?" Fiona backed her truck out onto the road, and put it into drive for the short trip home.

"I was thinking about that. I wonder if he did witness Prudence's murder and the murderer killed him so he wouldn't talk."

"Or, maybe he was the one who killed her, and then someone killed him for revenge."

"Like who?"

"Maybe Ed. Maybe he really did love her?"

Morgan pursed her lips. "Maybe. Or, it might not have anything to do with Prudence's murder. Jolene said he was a bad apple and into some shady stuff. Maybe one of his deals went bad."

"I can't believe Overton was trying to pin it on us. He really has it in for us ... well mostly for you. Why do you think that is?"

Morgan shrugged. "Who knows? I get the feeling he's had his eyes on us, watching us, since he came to town and investigated Mom's death. It's creepy."

Fiona sighed as she pulled into their driveway. "Well, I guess there is nothing we can do except try to get a good night's sleep. Tomorrow I have to get some of my projects at the shop out of the way so I can get Anastasia's set done by Friday. Tomorrow night Jake and I are supposed to meet with Cal to see if anyone has tried to pawn or sell Prudence's necklace. Wanna come?"

Morgan glanced sideways at her, a smile tugging the corners of her lips. "Oh, I'd love to but I can't."

Fiona's brow creased wondering what Morgan found so amusing. "Okay, I'll just go with him then. Maybe Cal will have a lead on the jewelry and Jake will have a better idea of who killed Josh Gray ... and why."

192

Chapter Twenty Three

Fiona felt a blast of cold air as Jake held the door of *Reed Pawn and Antiques* open for her. She slipped inside, rubbing her arms for warmth.

Her gaze went immediately to the front of the shop where she could see Cal squinting into a magnifying glass that he held about two inches away from a coin sitting on the glass display case that doubled as a counter. Cal looked up, smiling when he recognized her. His dimples and sparkling blue eyes highlighted the boyish good looks.

"Jeez, Cal, it's so cold in here, I can see my breath." She made a big show of blowing out for effect.

Cal laughed. "Sorry, sometimes it can get pretty heated in here when I am negotiating so I like to keep it frosty."

"How was your trip? Who was it this time? Sophie? Janice? Amanda?"

"Actually, none of the above." Cal grimaced at Fiona's raised brows. "Hey, I can't help it if my social calendar is too full.

It's a real problem trying to fit all the ladies in, you know."

Jake laughed. "Sounds like a problem I wouldn't mind having."

Fiona felt a momentary pang in her stomach. Jealousy? No, probably just indigestion from wolfing down a jalapeno burger at home before Jake picked her up.

"Cal, this is my friend Jake." Fiona ignored Cal's raised eyebrow and watched the two shake hands.

"So, what exactly is it you guys are looking for?"

"Apparently a necklace was taken from Prudence Littlefield when she was murdered. It was an initial necklace, a gold 'P'. We were wondering if you had heard of anyone trying to sell it. We're hoping to get a line on the killer to help out Morgan's case."

Cal looked out the window, his brow creased in thought. "You know, I think something like that came in while I was out. Let me check out back."

Cal disappeared through a door and returned a split second later with a small transparent bag in his hand. "Is this it? These two items came in together the other day."

Jake held the bag up and Fiona stood on her tiptoes to peer into it over his shoulder. She felt her breath catch when she saw it held a gold chain with a large 'P' in script and a chunky ring.

"Looks like it could be, but I'm not sure about the ring." Jake said.

Cal put a black velvet jeweler's square on the top of the glass display case and emptied the pieces out onto it.

"The necklace and charm are both 18K gold and the ring is 14K." Cal read from the slip that had been in the bag.

"Ed said Prudence's necklace was 18K. Who consigned these?"

Cal glanced at the slip "Joshua Gray."

Fiona gasped. "Then he must have killed Prudence."

"Maybe," Jake said, "But what about the ring? It's way too big for Prudence and Ed didn't say anything about a ring being missing."

Fiona bent down to get a better look at the ring. It had what looked like a family crest on it — a shield, a crow and two sheaves of wheat crossed in an X."

"Maybe he stole it from someone else."

"Maybe. I'll call into the station and see if anything like that has been reported stolen." Jake looked at Cal. "You better set these aside. They may be part of a police investigation."

Calvin raised his brows and Jake added. "Besides, your consigner was found dead last night, so I don't think he'll be needing the money."

***

"But why would Josh Gray want to kill Prudence Littlefield?" Fiona asked Jake as he pulled his Suburban away from the curb in front of Cal's store.

"I'm not sure. That's what we need to figure out."

"But now that we have this evidence, Morgan will be in the clear, right?"

"Not necessarily."

"What? But Josh had the necklace."

"That doesn't really prove anything. Someone could have given him the necklace, or he could have found it in the woods after the murder."

Fiona's heart dropped. She looked out the window at the passing scenery of downtown Noquitt. It was prime tourist season now and the streets were loaded with people walking down the sidewalks and browsing through the shops. But Fiona didn't see any of it. She was busy worrying about what was going to happen to Morgan.

Jake startled her out of her reverie by putting his hand on her knee.

"Don't worry, we'll get to the bottom of this and find the real killer."

Fiona's heart melted when she saw the genuine concern in his gray eyes.

"Thanks."

She noticed he didn't remove his hand and her heart started beating a little faster. A few minutes later, Morgan was the furthest thing from her mind as Jake pulled the truck into her driveway.

Fiona pushed the door handle. It opened smoothly this time, much to her disappointment. She was surprised when Jake turned off the engine. *Should she invite him in?*

"I'll walk you to the door," Jake said. "With all the things that are happening around you girls, you can't be too safe."

Fiona nodded and slipped out of the car, waiting for Jake to come round the front. Her heart skittered in her chest when he put his hand on the small of her back to lead her up the walkway to the porch.

They climbed the steps and she stopped at the door. She turned to say good night and realized he was standing close. Very close. Her stomach flip-flopped. The urge to run away swept over her. She felt like a teenager on her first date—awkward and unsure of what to do.

Jake must have been sure of what to do, though. He gently captured her slender wrists in his large hands kicking her pulse into overload. She wondered if he could feel it beating through her veins.

"Fiona, I want you to promise me that you and Morgan won't do anything ... you know, like go to question a possible killer ... without calling me first."

Fiona's mouth was too dry to speak so she simply nodded. He ran his hands from her wrists to her upper arms and she could feel the electricity buzzing between them.

Slowly, Jake leaned toward her. He gently brushed his lips against hers. Casual, at first as if he wasn't sure how she would react.

Fiona's breath caught in the back of her throat. The cool breeze of the ocean air, the chirping of peepers, and the spicy, sweet smell of Jake flooded her senses. She pressed closer to him, parting her lips.

Jake teased her lower lip with his tongue then slid it in further to meet her own sending jolts of pleasure through her body. She moaned and snaked her arms around his neck, pressing closer to him. How long had it been since someone had kissed her like this? Too long, Fiona thought, hoping Jake couldn't sense how badly she wanted him.

***

The feel of Fiona's body against his drove Jake almost to the brink of no return. The scent of her strawberry shampoo, silky feel of her skin and eager thrust of her tongue heated his veins.

He wrapped his arms around her waist and melded their bodies together, crushing his lips against hers almost hard enough to bruise them.

His hands caressed her back, as their tongues wrestled. She moved her hips closer to his and his hand instinctively cupped her bottom grinding her even closer. A deep moan ripped from his throat.

Jake knew he better back off before he couldn't stop himself. He was well aware of the disasters of taking things too far too soon and he wanted Fiona too badly to screw things up now.

He slid his hands back up to her hips. Pulling back he looked down at her upturned face. Her eyes still closed, lips swollen from their kiss. Feeling things stir in him that had lain dormant for a long time, he brushed a long red curl back from her face.

She opened her icy-blue eyes and Jake felt like he could get lost in them. He traced the curve of her jaw with his thumb.

"Maybe next time, we could have a more traditional date instead of doing detective work to track down a killer," Jake said.

She laughed and Jake placed a quick kiss on her forehead, then turned down the steps.

He looked back at her over his shoulder. "Don't forget, no detecting on your own."

She nodded and he watched her open the door and disappear into the house before he trotted to the Suburban.

Jake got in his truck and stared back at the house, his lips still burning from the kiss. He thought about the two murders and how Overton was hell bent on implicating one or more of the Blackmoore girls and his gut churned with worry.

He knew Fiona must be just as worried. Maybe more. He hoped she'd remember her promise not to investigate on her own, but he doubted her feisty, impulsive nature would let her. That was one of the things that attracted him to her even though, in this case, it could prove to be quite dangerous.

Jake sighed as he started the truck and put it in gear. All the more reason to step up his own investigation and find the real killer, fast. The stakes were too high for him to fail.

Chapter Twenty Four

Fiona floated through the next day, completing several orders for custom jewelry and dodging Morgan's probing questions.

When she and Morgan arrived home that evening, she felt like she was on top of the world ... well except for the little matter of two murders that the police seemed hell bent on accusing Morgan of.

"Let's order pizza and eat it out on the patio," Morgan said as they breezed through the large foyer, down the hall and into the kitchen.

"Sounds gre—"

Fiona's words froze in her throat when she saw the look on Celeste's face. Her sister was standing at the sink holding a letter, her skin almost as pale as the paper.

"What's wrong?" Morgan rushed over to Celeste.

"The tax bill came."

Fiona's heart lurched. With everything else going on she'd forgotten about the property taxes which were due in June. Their house and the cottage which housed *Sticks and Stones* had been handed down through the generations so they had no mortgage, but the property taxes were a killer—especially for the twenty-four room ocean side property.

"How much is it?" Celeste handed the paper over. Fiona's heart squeezed when she saw the amount.

"Do we have that much saved?"

Fiona shook her head. "I knew taxes were going up, but this is a big jump. We need another five thousand."

The girls stared at each other. "How are we going to get five thousand dollars in the next four weeks?"

The girls made enough to get by—pay the utilities, put food on the table and, usually, pay the taxes. But they had to scrape to save enough money for all that. There was no way they could come up with that much extra in such a short time.

Fiona felt tears prick the backs of her eyes. *Would they have to sell one of their properties to pay the taxes?*

"Meow."

Belladonna appeared at the bottom of the back stairs, staring at them with her ice-blue eyes. Fiona looked over, expecting the cat to trot to her food dish and demand someone fill it, but she stayed by the stairs, performing various gyrations of head butting and purring on the bottom step before looking back at the girls then running back up the stairs.

"That's it!" Morgan snapped her fingers. Celeste and Fiona looked at her with raised brows.

"We'll just go up into the attic and find something we can use to pay the taxes. You found that necklace up there, Fi, there's bound to be more valuable stuff up there."

"I don't know," Celeste glanced up at the ceiling. "I feel awful selling off our family heirlooms."

"Well, it's either that or sell the house. I say we take a look." Morgan started for the stairs.

Fiona exchanged a look with Celeste, shrugged and then followed Morgan.

"Let's look around the area where you found the necklace. Maybe there is more jewelry near it." Morgan stepped aside for Fiona to lead the way.

"I think it was over here." Fiona started off toward the right.

Belladonna let out a meow over to their left and Fiona spun around. "No wait. It was over there." She recognized the window and rocking chair.

The girls picked their way over then started rummaging through boxes. They pawed through boxes of linens, old scrapbooks and even a pile of old newspapers.

"Is any of this stuff valuable?" Celeste pulled a lace doily out of a box.

"I don't know. Maybe we should get Cal to come and look through some of it. He has a good idea about antiques."

Fiona sneezed as a dust cloud flew up into her nose from an old wooden box. Too bad that was all that was in it. "I don't see any more jewelry," she said, her heart sinking as she turned around to scan the area.

Belladonna weaved her way from sister to sister meowing and purring. She made her way over to Celeste then scratched at her leg and took off into the depths of the attic.

"Ouch." Celeste bent down to rub her leg.

"Meow." Belladonna brought their attention to an old bookshelf over by the wall.

"Hey, is that where you found that old book?"

Fiona craned her neck, looking around the various boxes and pieces of furniture to where Celeste stood. "Yes, that's it on the shelf ... the one without a layer of dust."

She turned back to the task of looking for valuable jewelry while Celeste picked the book out and set it on the table.

Fiona and Morgan picked their way over toward Celeste, stopping to look in any boxes that piqued their interest.

"This book seems to be a journal from the 1700s," Celeste said.

"That's pretty darn old. It must be from the original relative that built this house." Morgan bent down picking up a small wooden box.

"Yeah, it looks like a journal of his sailing trips and some of the stuff he brought back. There's even some entries about building this house. At least I think. It's hard to decipher the writing."

Fiona had made her way over to Celeste. She glanced over her shoulder at the book. "I wonder what *that* is worth."

Celeste jerked her head up, a look of horror on her face. "We would never sell something like this, this is our family history."

Fiona glanced back at the bookshelf. "Well, there's a ton of them here." She squatted down looking at the titles.

"This case is full of journals, ledgers, town history books. Hey, this one looks interesting." She pulled out a book on the families of Noquitt and started to leaf through it.

"Hey guys. Don't forget were up here to find something we can sell to pay the taxes." Morgan pulled an oak bureau away from the wall and started opening the drawers.

Fiona was about to put the book back and help Morgan when something caught her eye. A family crest—exactly like the one on the ring Josh had consigned to Cal. She stared at it, her photographic memory bringing up the image of the ring she had looked at just the day before. Her eyes flew to the top of the page. Her heart jerked in her chest when she saw whose family crest it was.

Stark.

"Why would Joshua Gray have a ring with the Stark family crest on it?" She looked up at her sisters who shrugged in unison.

A noise at the entrance to the attic caught their attention. All three of them swiveled their heads in that direction. Jolene stood at the top of the stairs, a piece of paper in her hand.

"I think I have a pretty good idea."

Chapter Twenty Five

Jake bent over the plain manila envelope that held Josh Gray's autopsy report and studied the notes from the medical examiner. Josh had been killed with a seven inch knife just like the M.E. had said on the scene. But what he didn't say on the scene was that Josh's septum had been ripped. Like someone had pulled something out of his nose. Like the nose ring they had found at the scene of Prudence's murder.

Jake rubbed the stubble on his face wishing he had found that nose ring in an official capacity. The nose ring combined with the jewelry Josh had consigned to Cal would have made powerful evidence that Josh killed Prudence. But now it was too late to admit the nose ring, unless he went back and planted it at the scene and somehow got Overton to agree to going over there again. That wasn't likely to happen.

At least he'd been able to log the jewelry from Cal's using the proper procedures. Too bad that ring hadn't been reported stolen.

Knowing where the ring came from could be a vital clue.

With the evidence, Jake was sure Gray had killed Prudence. But why? And then, who had killed Gray? And why?

Jake flipped the folder shut with a sigh. He got up from his desk making his way over to the coffee station just outside Overton's office. He had been trying to keep tabs on Overton and had discovered the best way was to linger at the coffee area since Overton had such a big mouth, he could be heard easily outside his office.

Jake peeked through an opening in the blinds that shielded Overton's office from the squad room. The Sheriff sat in his chair, feet up on the desk, toothpick in his mouth and phone pressed to his ear. Jake slowly poured thick, black sludge from the coffee pot into his mug.

"I'm telling you, those girls have something to do with these murders." Overton's voice wafted out of his office. Jake strained to hear while he slowly opened the creamer and poured it in his coffee.

"I think the oldest one killed Littlefield, but Gray must have seen her and she had to silence him. Her and the redhead were probably in on that one together."

Jake poured some sugar into his cup.

"I don't care how long their family has been in town."

Jake picked up a wooden stirrer and stirred his coffee, mindless of everything else except Overton's voice.

"I want a search warrant issued A.S.A.P—I'm sure they have vital evidence hidden somewhere on that property."

Jake thought about the nose ring on the kitchen counter and the scarf in Fiona's room. If Overton got that warrant, the girls could be screwed.

He pulled out his cell phone and bolted for his office.

Fiona didn't answer, so he tried Morgan. No answer. He slammed the phone shut, his heart pounding in his chest. Where were they?

His eyes darted around the office. He was on duty, and, technically not supposed to leave the station unless he was dispatched on a call, but screw it. He had to warn Fiona and Morgan. He grabbed his gun, shoved his chair back and ran out to his car.

Chapter Twenty Six

"I don't know if this is such a good idea," Morgan whispered to Fiona.

"If what Jolene found on the computer is true, then this is our best bet for catching the killer and finally proving you didn't do it."

"It seems pretty dangerous. Maybe we should have waited until Jake could come."

The promise she made to Jake flitted across Fiona's mind, but she knew he was on duty tonight and this couldn't wait. Hopefully he wouldn't have to come and arrest her for what she was about to do.

The back door to the house opened highlighting the silhouette of Eli Stark in the light streaming out from the kitchen.

Fiona crouched down even lower behind the bush holding her breath, praying Eli wouldn't spot her and Morgan on the other side of the driveway. Glancing over at her sister who wore an all-black outfit, hair stuffed up under a black baseball cap identical to hers, she realized she needn't have worried. It was a moonless night and the girls were all but invisible.

Stark got in his Black Lexus SUV and drove away. Fiona crept out from behind the bush quietly making her way over to the door. Taking a set of jeweler's tools from her pocket, she worked on the lock.

"Just how do you know how to pick a lock, anyway?" Morgan glanced around the yard nervously.

"I looked it up on the internet." Fiona shrugged. She'd never tried to pick a lock before, but it had looked easy and she already had the tools.

The door clicked then swung open and Fiona let out her breath. They tip toed into the house, carefully closing the door.

The house was dark. Fiona turned on her small flashlight sweeping it around the room. The kitchen of the small bungalow smelled like greasy fried food but was neat and tidy.

Who knew Eli was such a neat-nick?

A small table sat in one corner and the counters were bare. A dinner plate, silverware and a glass were stacked neatly in the sink.

Fiona made her way over to the knife rack while Morgan opened the drawers.

"Find anything?" Morgan asked.

"No, but I guess it's probably not the kind of knife he would keep in the kitchen."

"Yeah, let's look for an office or something That seems like a more likely place."

Fiona placed the knife rack exactly where she had found it and followed Morgan into the living room, then up the stairs, her heart leaping up into her throat at every creak and groan of the steps.

They found his office on the right. Morgan went over to the window and pulled the shades shut so no one would see their flashlights from outside. The girls started opening drawers and searching surfaces.

Fiona swept her flashlight across the room. The light fell on a big oak filing cabinet on the far wall. "I'm going to check out this filing cabinet."

"I'll go through the bookshelf over there by the door. Maybe he hid the knife behind a book or something."

Fiona grasped the filing cabinet handle and pulled, relieved when it opened smoothly. She pushed the files to the back of the drawer and looked underneath them. Nothing. Then she started to fan through the files, the knife could be inside any one of them.

Her heartbeat picked up as she glanced at the file tabs. One was labeled 'Blackmoore'.

Was Eli keeping a file on them?

She saw another one labeled 'Overton'. Clearly Eli was up to something. She started to flip through Overton's file trying to figure out what it was. She was so engrossed in her task that she was oblivious to everything else.

A frightened squeak sounded behind her. She whirled around. Her heart froze.

Eli was standing just inside the doorway, his hand over Morgan's mouth, a knife to her throat. A seven inch serrated knife with a fancy hilt. Just like the one that had killed Josh Gray.

"You'd love to see what's in that file, wouldn't you?" He sneered at Fiona.

Fiona's heart pounded in her chest as he advanced toward her, dragging Morgan with him. Morgan's eyes darted around the room in panic.

She dropped the file holding up her hands. "Let Morgan go."

Eli snickered. "Let her go? I don't think so." He tightened his grip on Morgan and Fiona's heart jerked at the muffled noise her sister made behind his hand.

Fiona's back was against the filing cabinet and she had nowhere to go. Her eyes searched the room frantically for some sort of weapon.

"Get the duct tape out of the bottom drawer." Eli indicated the bottom drawer of the filing cabinet with his foot. Fiona bent down as slow as she could, stalling for time.

"Hurry up!" Eli kicked the drawer causing Fiona to jump back. Instead of intimidating her as he intended, it only served to piss her off. Apparently Eli didn't know not to mess with a redhead that had a feisty temper.

She narrowed her eyes up at him. "Is that the knife you killed Josh Gray with?"

Eli snickered. "Well, aren't you the clever one? How did you figure it out? I suppose it doesn't matter now since I'll be killing you and your sister with the knife, too."

"So, you did kill him."

Eli nodded. "Little shit thought he could blackmail me. I showed him what for."

Fiona thought he almost looked proud of himself. "You hired him to kill Prudence and he threatened to tell."

"I paid him good money but he kept coming back for more, over and over. I just couldn't have that. So I took care of business."

"Well, it won't do you much good, the police know all about everything and they have proof so, even if you kill us, you'll get caught."

Eli pushed his chest out. "Ha! That's your mistake. I've got Overton in my pocket. He'll never prosecute me."

"I wasn't talking about Overton. I sent the information to the Fed's and they are very interested in what you have been doing." Fiona lied. Her heart pounded against her rib cage— this was her only chance.

Eli narrowed his eyes. She could almost see the wheels turning inside his head wondering if she told the truth.

Fiona saw him loosen his grip on Morgan. Adrenalin shot through her body. She grappled behind her, grabbing onto the cast iron doorstop she'd seen earlier.

She swung her hand up, shooting up from her squatting position at the same time to put as much force behind it as she could.

Eli threw his arm up instinctively to defend himself.

Morgan jerked away to the side.

Fiona felt the doorstop connect with Eli's forearm. Disappointment shot through her, she had aimed for his head. Hitting his forearm wouldn't be enough to knock him out. She had the doorstop raised high over her head for another attempt when a voice yelled from the doorway.

"Drop it and put your hands up!"

Fiona dropped the doorstop like a hot potato and put her hands up in the air, palms out.

"Not you." Jake stood in the doorway, Brody Hunter behind him, their guns raised and trained on Eli.

"Him." He said jerking his head toward Eli who had already dropped the knife and had his arms raised.

Fiona felt the tension drain from her body. She put her hands down and rushed over to Morgan who stood on the other side of the room rubbing a small nick on her neck.

"Are you okay?" her heart clenching at the small drop of blood.

"I'm fine." Morgan smiled at her. "I can't believe you got him to admit everything."

Behind them Brody and Jake were subduing a frantic Eli. Eli kicked and yelled about Overton and lawyers while they struggled to get him into the handcuffs.

Fiona's stomach dropped when Overton appeared in the doorway. *Would he ignore the evidence and make them let Eli go?*

Fiona pointed to the knife on the floor. "Eli had the knife he used to kill Josh Gray and he was planning on using it on us."

Overton's eyes went from the knife to Eli. His face looked haggard and worn. His shoulders sagged. He motioned for someone to put the knife in an evidence bag.

"Eli Stark, you're under arrest for the murder of Joshua Gray." Overton turned to Brody. "Get him out of here."

Eli stared at Overton, rage filling his beady, black eyes.

"You won't get away with this! I'll tell them everything I know about you! I'm not going down alone!" He screamed as Brody dragged him from the room.

Overton looked at Fiona and Morgan with disgust. "I guess you girls got your way ... this time." He shoved a toothpick into his mouth, turned on his heel and headed out of the room.

Morgan looked at Fiona. "I guess an apology was too much to expect."

Fiona's heart clenched when she saw Jake coming toward them.

"Are you okay?" His gray eyes studied both women with concern.

Fiona and Morgan nodded.

Jake sighed. "Thank god."

Fiona's heart skittered in her chest as he gathered her into his arms, bending to kiss her forehead.

"How did you know to come here?" Morgan asked.

"I went to your house. Jolene told me everything. She's pretty good with the computer. We could use someone like her down at the station ... if I'm even still employed there."

"I hope you didn't put your job at risk for us."

"We caught the bad guy, and that's what counts. I don't think we'd have been able to do that if it wasn't for you and your sisters."

Jake loosened his grip on Fiona. Tilting her head back he looked straight into her eyes. "But I am a little miffed that you didn't keep that promise to call me."

Fiona blanched. "Sorry, I wanted to call, but I knew you were on duty ..."

Jake just nodded then pulled her close again.

"Well, I can see I'm going to have to keep a *very* close eye on you from now on."

Fiona snuggled closer. A warm, satisfied glow spread through her veins. Having Jake Cooper keep a close eye on her was something she wouldn't mind, one bit.

Epilogue

Morgan Blackmoore tapped her finger lightly on the counter barely registering the low buzz of voices behind her in the crowded coffee shop as her mind raced over the events of the past few days.

"Here you go." Felicity handed Morgan a tray full of hot coffee and tea. Morgan turned and walked toward the large table where Fiona, Jake, Jolene, Celeste and Cal were seated.

"I still don't understand why Eli wanted to frame Morgan." Celeste said to Jake as she accepted the tea from Morgan with a nod of thanks.

"Actually, he was killing two birds with one stone, so to speak. He wanted Prudence out of the way so Ed would sell him their land and he figured if Morgan went to jail, the rest of the Blackmoore's would be eager to sell him the land where *Sticks and Stones* is since they'd have less income and more legal fees." Jake took a latte from the tray, handing it to Fiona before grabbing a coffee for himself.

"But what about the newt?"

"That was just luck on Eli's part. He was in the cafe and heard the exchange between Morgan and Prudence. He had already arranged for Josh to kill Prudence and he knew newts were plentiful in the woods so he simply called Josh and had him add that little twist."

"He'd already planned to plant the scarf, so the newt was just a bonus." Fiona added. "The whole town knows about our ongoing feud with Prudence so he figured they'd just think Morgan finally got fed up and snapped."

"So, if Eli thought putting me in jail would cause financial hardship, he must have known about our trouble with the taxes." Morgan's brow creased as she wondered how he knew.

"Sure, it's easy enough to figure out what we make for income and do the math." Jolene shrugged.

"Speaking of which." Cal pulled a check out of his shirt pocket and pushed it across the table to Morgan. "I found someone who was happy to buy that necklace."

Morgan's eyes widened when she looked at the check. "That's almost twice what we need for the taxes."

Cal leaned back in his chair smiling around the coffee stirrer he was chewing on.

Morgan looked at him suspiciously. "Cal, I hope this generous buyer isn't really you just giving us money."

The deep timber of Cal's laugh echoed across the restaurant causing four women at the next table to glance over and ogle him, which wasn't really any surprise to Morgan.

Since they were teens, Cal had been like a magnet to women. He had quite a reputation as a playboy but along with being handsome, smart and funny, Cal was also a nice guy that would do anything for his friends. Including disguising a gift of money as a sale of jewelry to make sure those friends didn't object.

He held is hands up. "No, it wasn't me. I swear. It was a real buyer and she's

229

interested in buying more if you have it. Any time you guys want to take another peek in the attic I'd be happy to help you identify some of the good stuff."

Morgan glanced around at her sisters. They had made a pact to keep as much of the family junk as possible ... they wouldn't be venturing into the attic unless they got desperate again.

"We'll keep you in mind. Hopefully we won't need to resort to that. I'm just glad we can put this whole thing behind us."

"We have Jolene to thank for that," Fiona said looking at her younger sister proudly. "If she didn't hack into Josh's accounts and trace the money to Eli, we might never have put it together."

"That took some skill. I think Jolene has quite a talent for computer work *and* detective work." Jake turned to Jolene. "You should really think about pursuing that."

Morgan watched a pink blush creep over Jolene's cheeks. "Well, actually, I did sign up for a class in computer forensics over the summer."

"That's great!" Morgan felt proud of her younger sister, she really *was* growing up.

"I've been wanting to get into law enforcement since I saw what a crappy investigation Overton did with Mom's death and I love computers so ..." she shrugged taking a sip of coffee.

"Speaking of Overton, I noticed Eli had a file on him in his office. Do you know what was in there?" Fiona asked Jake.

Jake shook his head. "The files from his office mysteriously disappeared." He lowered his voice and leaned in closer to the table. "I know Overton is up to something, but I just can't put my finger on it."

"Eli did say he had Overton in his pocket, whatever that means," Morgan said.

Jake narrowed his eyes. "It's more than just Eli. Something is off about him and I'm not going to stop until I find out what it is ... well after I get back from administrative leave, that is."

Morgan felt her stomach churn. Overton had put Jake on "administrative leave" for two weeks because he had left the station without getting dispatched on a call first. If Jake hadn't left when he did, Morgan and Fiona might be dead.

"That's so unfair he did that," Morgan said shaking her head.

"That's okay. It will give me some extra time to spend relaxing." Jake put his hand over Fiona's. The pointed look he gave Fiona and the subsequent blush on her cheeks left little room to wonder what he meant by "relaxing".

Morgan felt a tug in her gut. She used to be that happy with Luke. *Would she ever feel that again?* She was glad Fiona had moved on from her heartbreak with Kevin and found someone else. If she could do it, maybe Morgan could too.

She glanced out the window at the main street of Noquitt, busy with cars and pedestrian traffic. Her eyes went wide, her heart jerking in her chest when she thought she saw a familiar figure.

Could it be? She leaned closer to the window, squinting to get a better look but he had disappeared into the crowd.

"What's the matter, you look like you saw a ghost?" Fiona's voice laced with concern pulled her attention back to the table.

"Oh, it's just ... I thought I saw ... Luke Hunter." She glanced back out the window.

"What? I thought he was off fighting bad guys or capturing pirates or something." Celeste craned her neck to look in the direction of Morgan's attention.

"Yeah, it was probably just someone that looked like him." Morgan settled back in her chair not sure if the odd feeling in her gut was anger, relief or disappointment.

"Well, here's a toast to freedom and an uneventful and relaxing summer." Fiona raised her coffee cup to the middle of the table. The rest of them joined in, everyone tapping the lips of their paper cups together.

Morgan was all for having an uneventful summer. She'd had enough excitement these past two weeks to last a lifetime. The only problem was, she had a tingle in her gut that told her the rest of the summer was going to be anything but uneventful. And her gut feelings were usually right.

She brought the tea cup up to her lips. The cinnamon scent of herbal tea soothed her senses. Sitting back in her chair, she looked around the table at her smiling family and friends. Maybe this time, her gut would be wrong. She certainly hoped so.

After all, what more could possibly happen?

The End.

A Note From The Author

I hope you enjoyed reading this book as much as I enjoyed writing it. As you might have guessed, I have a whole series planned about the Blackmoore sisters filled with mystery, murder and romance, so stay tuned!

The setting for this book series is based on one of my favorite places in the world - Ogunquit Maine. Of course, I changed some of the geography around to suit my story, and changed the name of the town to Noquitt but the basics are there. Anyone familiar with Ogunquit will recognize some of the landmarks I have in the book.

The house the sisters live in sits at the very end of Perkins Cove and I was always fascinated with it as a kid. Of course, back then it was a mysterious, creepy old house that was privately owned and I was dying to go in there. I'm sure it must have had an attic stuffed full of antiques just like in the book!

Today, it's been all modernized and updated and I think you can rent it out for a summer vacation. In the book the house looks different and it's also set high up on a cliff (you'll see why in a later book) where in real life it's not. I've also made the house much older to suit my story.

Also, if you like cozy mysteries, you might like my book *"Brownies, Bodies & Bad Guys"* which is part of my Lexy Baker cozy mystery series. I have an excerpt from it at the end of this book.

This book has been through many edits with several people and even some software programs, but since nothing is infallible (even the software programs) you might catch a spelling error or mistake and, if you do, I sure would appreciate it if you let me know - you can contact me at lee@leighanndobbs.com.

Oh, and I love to connect with my readers so please do visit me on facebook at *https://www.facebook.com/leighanndobbsbooks* or at my website *http://www.leighanndobbs.com* Are you signed up to get notifications of my latest releases and special contests? Go to: *http://www.leighanndobbs.com/newsletter* and enter your email address to signup - I promise never to share it and I only send emails every couple of weeks so I won't fill up your inbox.

About The Author

Leighann Dobbs discovered her passion for writing after a twenty year career as a software engineer. She lives in New Hampshire with her husband Bruce, their trusty Chihuahua mix Mojo and beautiful rescue cat, Kitty. When she's not reading, gardening or selling antiques, she likes to write romance and cozy mystery novels and novelettes which are perfect for the busy person on the go.

Find out about her latest books and how to get discounts on them by signing up at:

http://www.leighanndobbs.com/newsletter

Connect with Leighann on Facebook and Twitter

http://facebook.com/leighanndobbsbooks

http://twitter.com/leighanndobbs

More Books By This Author:

Lexy Baker
Cozy Mystery Series
* * *

Killer Cupcakes
Dying For Danish
Murder, Money and Marzipan
3 Bodies and a Biscotti
Brownies, Bodies & Bad Guys
Wedded Blintz

Blackmoore Sisters
Cozy Mystery Series
* * *

Dead Wrong
Dead & Buried
Dead Tide
Buried Secrets

Contemporary
Romance
* * *

Sweet Escapes
Reluctant Romance

***

Excerpt From Brownies, Bodies and Bad Guys:

Lexy sat at one of the cafe tables next to the picture window in her bakery, *The Cup and Cake,* admiring how the princess cut center stone of her engagement ring sparkled in the midmorning sunlight. She sighed with contentment, holding her hand up and turning the ring this way and that as she marveled at the rainbow of colors that emerged when it caught the light at different angles.

Her thoughts drifted to her fiance, Jack Perillo. Tall, hunky and handsome, her heart still skipped a beat when he walked in the room even though they'd been dating for over a year. Lexy had met Jack, a police detective in their small town, when she'd been accused of poisoning her ex-boyfriend. She'd been proven innocent, of course, and she and Jack had been seeing each other ever since. And now they were getting married.

Movement on the other side of the street caught her attention, pulling her away from her thoughts. Her eyes widened in surprise— it was Jack! *What was he doing here?*

Lexy felt a zing in her stomach. Jack wasn't alone. Lexy's eyes narrowed as she craned her neck to get a better look. He was with a woman. A tall, leggy blonde who was clinging to him like tissue paper clings to panty hose.

Lexy stood up pressing closer to the window, her joy in the ring all but forgotten. Her heart constricted when she saw how the leggy blonde was pawing at Jack, giggling up into his face. *Who the hell was she?* They looked very familiar with each other. Clearly Jack knew her ... and it seemed he knew her well.

Jack and the blonde started to walk down the street, out of view. Lexy pushed herself away from the window, stumbling over a chair in her haste to get to the doorway. She spun around, righting the chair, then turned, sprinting toward the door.

She reached out for the handle, jerking back in surprise as the door came racing toward her, almost smacking her in the face.

Standing in the doorway was her grandmother, Mona Baker, or Nans as Lexy called her. But instead of her usual cheery appearance, Nans looked distraught. Lexy could see lines of anxiety creasing her face and her normally sparkly green eyes were dark with worry.

Lexy's stomach sank. "Nans, what's the matter?"

"Lexy, come quick," Nans said, putting her hand on Lexy's elbow and dragging her out the door. "Ruth's been arrested!"

###

"Arrested? For what?" Lexy asked, as Nans propelled her down the street toward her car.

"Nunzio Bartolli was found dead. They think Ruth might have something to do with it!"

Lexy wrinkled her brow. Ruth was one of Nans's best friends. They both lived at the retirement center in town and along with two of their other friends, Ida and Helen, they amused themselves by playing amateur detective solving various crimes and mysteries. The older women were full of spunk and could be a handful, but Lexy had a hard time believing any of them would be involved in a murder. They thrived on *solving* murders, not *committing* them.

"What? How would Ruth even know him?" Lexy opened the door to her VW beetle and slipped into the driver's seat as Nans buckled up in the passenger seat.

"Nunzio was a resident at the Brook Ridge Retirement Center."

Lexy raised her brows. "He was? I heard he had ties to organized crime."

"Well, I don't know about that. He seemed like a nice man." Nans shrugged, then waved her hand. "Now let's get a move on!"

Lexy pulled out into the street, glancing over at the area where she had seen Jack. She slowed down as she drove by, craning her neck to look down the side street where she thought they had gone, but they were nowhere to be seen.

"Can you speed it up? Ruth needs us." Nans fidgeted in the passenger seat.

"Right. Sorry." Lexy felt a pang of guilt. Of course, helping Ruth was more important than finding out what Jack was up to. It was probably nothing but her overactive imagination anyway. Lexy decided to push the leggy blonde from her mind and focus on Ruth.

"So what happened?"

"I'm not really sure. Ida said the police knocked on Ruth's door early this morning and took her in," Nans said, then turned sharply in her seat. "We should call Jack and see if he can help her. Why didn't I think of that before?"

Lexy's stomach clenched at the sound of her fiance's name. She wasn't sure if she wanted to call Jack right now, especially with the image of him and the blonde fresh in her mind. *Should she confront him or let it slide?*

If it was innocent, which it probably was, she'd just make a fool out of herself by confronting him. It was probably a good idea to let some time pass before she talked to him. Lexy was afraid her impulsive nature might cause her to blurt something out she might regret later.

"Hopefully, he'll be at the station. I should call Cassie back at the bakery though, and tell her I've gone out for a while. She'll probably be wondering where I disappeared to." Lexy picked up her cell phone just as she pulled into the parking lot at the police station.

Nans jumped out of the car before she even had it in park. "I'll see you in there."

Lexy watched in amusement as the sprightly older woman sprinted into the station, her giant purse dangling from her arm. She felt sorry for any officer that might try to prevent her grandmother from seeing Ruth.

She made a quick call to Cassie, letting her know where she was and that she'd fill her in later. Then she made her way into the lobby behind Nans.

Nans was talking to Jack's partner, police detective John Darling, who nodded at Lexy as she joined them.

"Ruth isn't arrested!" Nans smiled at Lexy.

Lexy raised an eyebrow at John.

"We just had her in for questioning," John explained.

"Why?"

John rubbed his chin with his hand. "We found her fingerprints and some of her personal effects in Nunzio Bartolli's condo."

Nans gasped. "What? How would those get in there?"

John winked, pushing himself away from the wall he was leaning against. "You'll have to ask Ruth that."

Lexy stared after him as he walked over to the reception desk, his long curly hair hung in a ponytail down his back which swung to the side as he leaned his tall frame over the counter to look at something on the computer. "Actually, she's free to go now. I'll bring her out here if you guys want."

"Please do," Nans said, then turned to Lexy. "Isn't that wonderful? I was so worried."

Lexy nodded as she watched John disappear through the door that led to the offices inside the station. John and her assistant Cassie had been married this past spring and she'd gotten to know him fairly well. She wondered if she should ask him if he knew anything about the blonde she had seen Jack with but didn't want to seem like she was prying into Jack's business.

Lexy shook her head. She needed to stop thinking about the blonde. She trusted Jack. They were getting married, for crying out loud, and she didn't want to be one of those wives who kept her husband on a short leash. The best thing for her to do was to forget all about it.

The door opened and Ruth came out. Nans rushed over giving her a hug. Lexy felt her shoulders relax, relieved that Ruth wasn't in trouble.

"Oh, thanks for coming," Ruth said to Nans and Lexy.

"No problem," Lexy said. "Shall we go? I can drive you guys back to the retirement center, if you want."

"That would be wonderful," Nans said as the three of them made their way to the door. Lexy held it open for the two older women, then followed them out into the summer sunshine.

Ruth breathed in a deep breath of fresh air. "It's good to be outside. For a while there I was a little worried I might be spending my golden years in a cell."

"Why would you think that? Surely you had nothing to do with Nunzio's murder?"

Nans raised her eyebrows at Ruth as they walked to Lexy's car.

"Of course I didn't! But they did have some evidence that pointed to me," Ruth said, as she folded herself into Lexy's back seat.

"That's what John said." Lexy slipped into the driver's seat angling the rear view mirror so she could look at Ruth. "What was that all about?"

Lexy saw Ruth's cheeks turn slightly red.

Nans turned in her seat so she could look at Ruth, too. "John said they found your fingerprints and personal effects in Nunzio's condo. How is that possible?"

Ruth turned an even darker shade of red and looked down at her lap, pretending to adjust her seatbelt. "I was in his condo."

"What?" Nans and Lexy said at the same time.

Ruth looked up. Her eyes met Lexy's in the mirror then slid over to look at Nans. "I was seeing Nunzio. Actually, I went there quite regularly. So, naturally, my fingerprints were all over his condo. I was there last night and I must have left a pair of earrings there that the police were somehow able to trace to me."

Nans gasped. "You were there last night? The night he was murdered?"

Ruth nodded. "Yes, I was. But don't worry. I assure you Nunzio was *very* much alive when I left."

Made in the USA
Columbia, SC
24 September 2023

23328451R00137